Red Warp

Don DeBon

Red Warp

Don DeBon

First Printing
Copyright © 2013 Don DeBon

ISBN 978-0-9881783-6-6
ISBN 978-0-9881783-2-8 (e-book)

Dedicated to the one special woman in my life who convinced me to take up my pen again.

Not to mention my wonderful editors. This book would not have been possible without you.

Contents

— 1 —

She looked around the room and sighed flicking her long red hair over her shoulders as she stood up. She knew that it would drain her beyond normal limits, already being so very tired, but there was little choice. They would be back soon and then her time would be up. They wanted her power, or thought her insane. While most didn't really believe, they would soon! And to think she came to *help* them! She looked around the small room again. She picked up the four heavy wooden chairs and placed them on the table that took up almost the entire space.

She sighed again and pulled the zipper of her skintight black bodysuit all the way up, past her neck. She hoped there was enough room. She had never done it in such a small space before. Looking off into the distance and with great concentration she began to run. In a circle . . . faster and faster. Air began to swirl around picking up several papers that were on the table and flung them into the wind. Faster and faster she ran. "I must *DO* this!" She muttered and increased her speed again. One of the chairs flew off and were now following her swept up in the whirlwind. A storm had formed. A storm of her own making.

1

And with the crack of thunder a bolt shot from the center and the room reeked of ozone. She increased her speed once more but began to feel the storm's draining effect and knew she was out of time.

With a loud *KABOOOM* that shook the whole building, a warp had formed. A rip in the very fabric of space and time. She knew there were only seconds before they came running in here. The table cracked, splintered, fell in upon itself, and disappeared as the warp grew gaining strength. A microsecond later the door burst open with armed men ready to do battle, but with the storm all they could do was hang on to the door frame as the great forces pulled them horizontal.

The warp was smaller than usual, but she could not go anymore. It was enough. She ran for it and jumped into the angry swirl of color. With a loud *CRASH* it closed in upon itself and instantly the wind died. People and the chairs fell to the floor with a *thud*.

Stars in a multitude of colors streamed past her vision. She knew they were not real stars but she was beyond what her mind could comprehend, making them look like stars.

As quick as it started, it stopped. She fell to the ground on a soft patch of grass. Gazing around she saw trees, lush streams and heard birds chirping in the background. She knew it was not a matter of *where* she was but *when*. She closed her eyes and muttered "I must rest" and fell into a deep sleep.

Red awoke with a start looking up to a dark sky filled with stars and half of a moon. How much time had passed? She gazed at her self illuminating watch and silently laughed. Without looking before she closed her eyes, there was no way to know how long she had been unconscious. Could be a few hours later or more than a day.

She straightened and felt every muscle in her body

complain all at once. Looking around the area where once a vast building stood, she was reminded how risky warping was, especially since she was on the third floor. Thankfully, the warp had drifted down a little or she could have died from the fall when she arrived here ... wherever here was. No, she corrected herself, *whenever*.

Red slowly got to her feet, listening to the crickets and bullfrogs in the distance, although she thought they sounded different for some reason. She sighed thinking how she was always called Red as far back as she could remember, which wasn't very far. There was a large gap in her memory and she didn't know why. Then her head spun, the world wobbled and she realized getting up right now was not such a good idea. She fell back to the ground asleep before her head touched the grass.

Red awoke to someone shaking her violently. She blinked trying to clear her vision. Then she saw the glint of a gun shoved into her face. "*WHO* are you! And where are we?" The man waved his gun around and shouted. "Answer me! I am not in the mood for games. The building is gone, everything is gone! Where are we!"

Her vision finally cleared, and she recognized him as one of the agents that came into the room right before she jumped. He must have traveled with her. This was a first. She looked around then back at him. "I ...I ...I don't know," she stammered.

Suddenly they heard a sound. An alien sound of something very large nearby. Her blood turned to ice. She went back all right, but way too much.

The man looked around momentarily forgetting Red entirely. "What in the world was that?!"

Red quickly shushed him. "Shut up you moron or we will be a meal. Now get off of me and put that gun away. If it goes off, we are dead."

"I want to–" he said with a confused look.

"Okay let me try this again. Do you want to live?"

He looked blankly at her for a second in a state of shock.

"Of course, what kind of question is that?"

"Then stop asking me stupid questions and do as I say and you might live to see tomorrow! You got that?"

He nodded slowly and got off of her and she leapt to her feet. She had been here before, and that was trying to see how far she could go. Dang them! If it wasn't for their interference in her concentration, the jump wouldn't have thrust them this far back!

The earth shook slightly as they felt a tremor. A small one, almost imperceptible, then the next one …stronger …the then the next even stronger yet.

"What is–"

Red covered his mouth. "Shut up! Do you want to get us killed?" she whispered. "Now follow me and for goodness' sake try to be quiet!" He holstered his gun, she grabbed his wrist, and they moved as quietly as they could to a thick patch of very large foliage she could just make out in the dim light. She jumped into the large ferns and pulled him in with her. Their noses wrinkled as the ferns strong scent covered them. Red just hoped it would be enough. The earth shook again more violently this time as a giant foot of a Tyrannosaurus rex landed very close to them. The beast looked around sniffing the air then leaned down to where they were hiding and sniffed again, looking confused. His head bobbed up again as he looked around. Then he put his snout down and began to push into the ferns when a loud sound froze him into place. He raised his head and gave an angry retort to the air and took off in the direction of the challenge.

"That was–"

Red slapped her hand over his mouth. "Do you ever shut up?" she whispered. "Give it another minute or two then we can move." After a few minutes, which seemed like hours in their cramped location under the ferns, she stood up. "Should be clear now. I am sure he took off after the challenger at full speed and won't be back now."

The man stood up his face glistened in the dim moonlight wet from sweat or the ferns, Red couldn't tell which. "What was that?"

"Tyrannosaurus rex. I'm sure you have heard of them."

"Of course I have heard of them! But they are long dead. So are we on some kind of movie set?"

Red snorted. "Don't I wish!"

"Well then where are we?"

Red glared at him as she sat down on a large rock nearby. "Isn't it obvious?"

The man looked blank. "No."

"Okay let me try this again, really really slowly. That was a real dinosaur. A Tyrannosaurus rex, now think for a moment. What does that mean?"

"We went back in time?"

Red raised her arms looked to the sky. "Thank you God, yes he can be taught!" She lowered her arms and jabbed a finger in the man's face. "Now if it wasn't for you, I wouldn't be in this situation."

"Because of me?" He said placing a hand on his chest. "I didn't do this to you!"

"You did! You broke my concentration! I came to try and help save your president, and what do I get? People calling me insane and think I am a terrorist. If I was a terrorist would I have been warning people? You government types have no sense at all."

"We broke your concentration?"

"Yes YOU! I should have normally spent an hour preparing

for that jump, instead I had to do it blind. I only wanted to jump a little bit not this freaking far!"

"And why do you keep saying we did this? I didn't do this to you."

"You are with the FBI aren't you?"

"Well yes–"

"Well then, who are *you*?" Red felt the idiocy of the question the second after she said it.

He stiffened. "Agent James Moknkin!"

"Oh full agent, eh? And where is your access badge?" She said pointing at his chest.

James looked down to see a ripped spot on his sport jacket where his badge once hung. "Well looks like it was taken off by a whirlwind that *someone* else made!"

"And how long have you been there?"

"My first day, I–"

Red snorted and shook her head. "Just great. All the agents in the world and I get stuck with a trainee in the distant past!"

"Hey, I will have you know I graduated first in my class!"

"Well excuuuuse me. But I bet your training never covered this!"

"Er … um … no. And how did you know the ferns would shield us?"

"I have been here before. Long ago. It was a mistake. At the time I was wondering how far I could go, I shouldn't have tried it. I learned a lot about dinosaurs that the paleontologists got totally wrong. Like these ferns act like Jurassic pepper. They don't smell anything other than the ferns for awhile, but it also can make them sneeze. And believe me you don't want to be sneezed on by a dinosaur, it is really disgusting."

"I see. Now could you please tell me who you are?"

Red snorted. "I think you already know."

James rolled his eyes. "No I don't. I don't know what your case was. They called an emergency and all agents on the floor were to report to holding room 3. I happened to be a few doors down and came running."

"Lucky you." Red said as she sat down on a large rock and rubbed her sore muscles.

"Yeah lucky me," He sighed.

"Well I am Red."

"Red …?"

"Yes Red."

"That is all?"

"Yes that is all I can remember. As far as I know I have always been called Red."

"You have amnesia?"

"Well, I'm not sure. I don't have any memories past 8 years ago. What happened before then I don't know." She shrugged and stretched cracking her back.

"I see. Now can you please get us back?"

"I'm not sure I can."

"WHAT! What do you mean you are not sure? You got us here!" James said a little more loudly than he intended.

"Well to be honest I don't know exactly how I do what I do. Only that I can and it takes a great deal of concentration and energy. And if I don't, then very odd things can happen, like this." She paused a moment to gesture to the surrounding land.

"But you said you were here before?" James said sitting down next to her on the large rock.

"Yes. I shouldn't have tried it though. I was seeing how far I could go. It was a mistake. But a bigger one than I thought. You must understand, then like now, I managed to get here in one jump. But getting back was difficult. It took over twenty jumps."

"Twenty? Twenty of those ... storms?"

"Yes. And I traveled alone. In fact I don't know how you managed to follow me. What was the last thing you remember?"

"Well ..." James looked off into the starry night that was starting to give way to morning. "As I said I heard the emergency call, and I came running into holding room 3. The door was gone, ripped right off its hinges, and I remember seeing a whirlwind. I tried to stop but couldn't. That is all until waking up here."

"Sounds like the combination of your motion and the storm carried you into the warp allowing you to follow me here. Amazing really, no one has ever followed me before." Red said as she watched the sun peek over the horizon gently waking everything around them.

"Have they ever tried?" James looked at her concerned.

"One did I think. But he never made it. Normally people are not around me when I jump. Safer for everyone."

"Well after experiencing this first hand, I have to agree."

Red jumped up from the rock and stretched again. "We need to get going. With the sun up we are sitting ducks out here in the open. We need to find better cover."

"Can't you get us back? You said it took you twenty jumps, but you did make it. Why don't we get started now?"

Red sighed and started walking towards what looked like caves in the distance. "Look, for one thing every jump drains me. The longer the jump the more of the drain. It may take me a few days before I am up to trying again. Perhaps longer. And secondly I don't know you. The FBI was going to lock me up as a security risk and you are part of the organization. So excuse me if I don't feel like helping you."

"Why did the bureau want to lock you up? What did you do?" James said as he followed along behind her and silently wished he had worn his black sneakers instead of his dress shoes, they were not the best in this environment.

"It is what I tried to do, rather than what I did."

"Tried to do?"

"Okay here goes, I saw the president die. This allowed the vice president to take over. Unfortunately this turned out to be very bad and the decisions he made lead to a full scale nuclear war in one hundred years time. There wasn't much left of the earth after that point. I tracked the start of the whole situation to this one point in time. I thought perhaps if I traveled back and warned the FBI they could avoid it. Of course, they didn't believe me. The problem is I gave them detailed information about the president over the next few days. Where he was, who was there, exact times and dates. Something that turned out to be classified information."

"Oh I see, so they thought you were a part of the situation instead of trying to help?"

"Exactly. I told them of my ability, but of course they didn't believe me. And at that point I think that even if they did, I would have been locked up to find out how I do it. I decided I needed to get out of there and fast. I had no intention of being a lab rat." They continued walking towards a group of rocky outcroppings in the distance. By this time the terrain had already changed from a soft grassy plain to jagged rocks laying haphazardly. James stumbled and Red sighed as she helped him, yet again, to his feet.

"Can we rest? We have come a long way. Surely we are safe now?"

Red rolled her eyes. "Not yet, once we get to those caves, then we can. We are still too exposed here. You don't know dinosaurs, they rarely give up once they get your scent. Well the carnivores anyway. The herbivores you only have to worry about them stepping on you." She pulled at James' arm. "Come on will you. I thought you said you were top of your class?"

"I was. But the training didn't include early Jurassic!"

When they finally reached one of the caves, they both collapsed on its dirt floor and James immediately removed his shoes to rub his aching feet. "I don't suppose you know where the closest restaurant is?"

"Sure, thousands of years in the future," Red chuckled. "But I think I can come up with something a little closer. I noticed a tree with fruits when we came in. I will go get some of them. Will you be okay?"

James nodded. "Yes I will be fine." He said sitting down on a large rock, patting it. "All the comforts of home."

Red smiled as she turned to leave. "I will be back."

A short time later Red appeared at the cave entrance carrying two large plum colored oblong objects. Both were larger than her hands and she had to carry one under each arm. "Here you are," she said handing him one, "but be careful, some inner pods are seeds and will break your teeth. Also, if you ever find some that look like these but are shiny, don't eat those. They will kill you in one bite."

"How do you know?" He said as he chewed the sweet fruit.

"I got lucky enough to watch something else take a bite. Believe me, you don't want to try it." Red said as she broke open her fruit and popped a small yellowish oblong piece into her mouth.

"Thanks, I will keep that in mind. You said you were here

before and it took twenty jumps to get back? Why so many?" James said as he finished the last of his fruit.

"Well, going forward is much more difficult than going backwards in time. I don't know why. But I do know it takes a lot more energy and concentration." Red raised her hand. "And before you ask, it still will be about another day before I can try. Believe me, I don't like being here in dinosaur world anymore than you do. But this is a lot better than Salem."

James eyes grew wide. "Salem?"

"Yes you know of the city right?"

"Of course, but how can you say this is better than Salem?"

Red laughed. "Okay, well in modern times I agree, but if you land in the middle of a witch trial looking like this from a storm what would you think just happened?"

"You are kidding? You were in Salem during the witch trials?"

"I wasn't there during the witch trials, I was the reason for them! Sadly I landed right at the feet of a judge. Of course he immediately called everyone around and shouted witch. And just my luck, he wasn't the only one that saw me land …"

3

Red groaned as she fought to stay conscious. She shook her head, which turned out to be a mistake. Her head thumped in loud protest and someone was screaming in her ear. Or was it nearby? She blinked again and again to clear her vision. She saw a man in black clothing yelling at her. She blinked again and saw him holding a …no it could be a …*Bible* in front of himself? She had made many jumps, but this was certainly turning out to be the most bizarre. Now if her ears would only stop ringing. Finally she could make out he was shouting "witch", and now others were rushing to his shouts. Red silently cursed. If only she wasn't so weak, she would be running away from these strange people, and fast.

Red looked up at the man and forced herself to sit up. Knowing she couldn't run she might as well try to appease them. "Sir, I don't know what the problem is. But could you please tell me where I am?"

The man's face grew fire red. "Like you don't know witch! There has been rumors that witches were in the area, which I discounted! What a mistake! Now I see you arrive by the eye of the devil himself! Red and full of flame it was! And even your dress shows your true nature. You shall be tried and convicted witch! Salem shall not make the same mistake again!"

"Salem? I am in Salem?" Red blinked. "This could not get any worse." But a second after she said it two strong men grabbed and forced her to her feet. "Please, I am no witch, I–"

"Silence witch! I William Stoughton know how to deal with you. Take her away and make sure her hands are bound so she can't enchant you."

"Yes sir." The men on either side of her said as they led her away.

Some hours later Red was feeling better. The rest had made a big difference. Her stomach rumbled but quickly quieted when she saw the food. Apparently they only fed witches moldy bread and stagnant water. She sighed and shoved the small metal plate aside. Its contents wasn't fit for a dog, much less a human. She looked around the small cell. Far too small to run in. It was barely large enough for the old cot she was on.

Red flopped back down on the greasy cot and sighed. She couldn't tell them she was from the future, or how she traveled, they would hang her for sure. Thinking back, was there any result other than death after one was accused of witch craft in Salem? Her blood went cold. No there wasn't. Once you were accused, the trial was a mere formality. She had to get away, but how? Then it came to her. A long shot but it might work. A smile crossed her face as she made her plans. "Yes this could work," she muttered. "It has got to."

Sunlight streamed into the bar covered window and gently woke Red from her restless sleep just as there was a rap on the other side. "Get up witch! The trial starts in thirty minutes. Here is your food." He said while shoving it through the space under the bars, then turned to leave pausing to laugh manically over his shoulder. "Enjoy."

Red looked at yet another plate of moldy bread and sighed. Then her eyes flashed with an idea. She picked up the slice of bread and ran her fingers over it. Faster and faster until it began to smoke from the friction. She smiled. "It will work." She muttered while her smile broadened.

A few minutes later the guard appeared, bound her hands and he along with two others, escorted her down the dusty streets to the court house. On lookers watched and chanted "witch witch witch" as she passed. Red shook her head. The ignorance of them astounded her. All she had read about how this was an example of extreme fanaticism was true. It was hard to believe that any sane human could condemn another so quickly without first researching and proving one way or the other. It was obvious that the modern justice system had used Salem as a model how not to be. Deep in her thoughts she stumbled and the one guard pulled the rope that bound her hands forcing her to the ground. He stood over her and shouted "Keep moving witch! Your delaying tactics won't work here! I have seen this all before."

"Delaying? Who is delaying?" she said aghast. "I tripped on–"

"Silence! Anything more and I will take care of your devil ways right here! Keep moving!" He said prodding her with a stick while giving the rope another yank.

Red opened her mouth to respond, then thought better of it. There was no reasoning with these people. It was often said one cannot reason with closed minds ... but these were so closed, locked, and lost that it would take a flashlight the size supernova to find the keyhole. Again she pitied these people. They were mostly doing this out of fear. Fear of what they didn't understand. She quickened her pace as not to give the guard another reason to flaunt his control. But Red would have the last laugh.

They soon entered the court house and Red was pushed into the one of the hard wooden chairs reserved for the accused. She looked around the simple design of the wooden structure. Most of the accounts she had read romanticized it giving much more detail and design than was actually here. "At least they did get the attitudes right," she muttered.

"What was that?" The guard closest to her said his face stormy.

"Nothing."

"Good. Now stand for the judge." He said yanking on the rope that bound her hands. As Red got to her feet, she saw a man in long plain black robes with a large white area around his neck enter the room step up and into the judge's booth and sit down.

Red recognized him instantly. The man she encountered first and accused her of witchcraft. "Just great. Could this get any worse?" she muttered.

"Be seated everyone. I am in a difficult position here. Since I am the first one that actually saw the witchcraft take place I have to state my account. However, I can't normally be a judge and do that as well. Sadly another judge is days away and since our law is we must have a trial within two days of witchcraft being seen, I must take both positions of prosecutor and judge. But I will restrict myself to the facts and not make any statements other than what I saw. The facts should speak for themselves. And in this unusual case, the jury will issue the sentence. Is everyone in agreement with this?"

The jury all nodded and a man on the end stood. "Your Honor, we the jury find this suggested course of action perfectly acceptable given the unusual situation. You have a good record and of course we all know you will leave the accounts before us as they happened."

"Yeah right," Red snorted.

The judge heard something and whirled to face her. "The witch will be silent and no further disruptions will be tolerated in this court! Anything more and you will be found in contempt!"

"What are you going to do? Kill me twice?" Red retorted.

The judge's face grew hotter than the sun. "You will find there are many ways to die. Some longer and more painful than others. Do I make myself clear?"

"Perfectly." Red said as she wiggled her hands inside her bonds.

The judge cleared his throat. "Now then, back to the business at hand. I the honorable William Stoughton saw this fall at my feet from the devils storm itself!" Pointing towards Red as he spoke.

"What was it like?" One of the spectators shouted.

"There will be no shouting in my court room." The judge said then looked towards the jury. "But the question is valid and I do want to give all the facts possible. It was like an angry eye at the center. I suspect it was the eye of the devil. The wind around it swirled and threw dust and dirt everywhere. A moment later this woman came through the eye and landed at my feet. Probably from hell itself! Now if that is not witchcraft I don't know what is!"

The jury applauded the judge's account. Red snorted and almost said *"Then you obviously don't know what witchcraft is."* But then after looking at the large brute of a guard ready to use his sizable club, she thought better of it. She continued to move her hands faster and faster in her bonds keeping them hidden under the old oak table in front of her.

The judge stood. "You have heard the evidence. Does the jury have a decision?"

A man at the end of the row of chairs with the jury stood. "We have your Honor. We the jury have found this woman guilty of witchcraft. As per our laws she is to be hanged at–"

The ropes holding Red's hands began to smoke. This part she had planned, but she had failed to notice that she was also rubbing the table. Suddenly the area of the table directly in front of her burst into flames! She was pulled back by one guard as another one dumped a bucket of water on the table instantly putting it out.

The judge stood. "So you like to play with fire? Can there be any doubt this is a witch? If you like fire so much you can die by it. The jury has already sentenced you to death, I will make it more appropriate! This witch is to be burned at the stake before nightfall!"

The spectators and jury were now chanting "Burn her! Burn her! Kill the witch! Kill the witch!"

"Guards, take this witch outside before she tries to burn something else and have the sentence ready to be carried out before nightfall. I don't want to take the chance she will enchant us again."

"Yes your Honor." They said in unison before pulling Red out of the courthouse and into the dirty street.

Red looked around and saw the gallows along the side being lined with easily burnable materials. Obviously they were intending to make a bonfire as quickly as they could. Then she noticed the sun was about to set. It would be night soon, no wonder everyone was hurrying.

By this time everyone from the courthouse had filed outside

and a large crowd had gathered shouting "Burn the witch! Burn the witch!" Several even spit at her although they didn't get close enough for their saliva to actually reach.

A few minutes later, with the bonfire ready to light, the judge raised his hands. "Citizens of Salem, we now condemn this witch to the evil from whence she came! Guards secure her to the post in the center!"

"Yes, your Honor." They said pulling Red up and tying her to the post that used to be gallows only a few moments ago.

The judge raised his arms again and shouted "Light it!" And several fire bearers stepped forward and threw their fire encased sticks into the wood and thatch at Red's feet.

Red shouted, "I am no witch and mark my words someday you will regret your actions of today and the innocent people you have killed in the name of justice!" As the flames grew higher she smiled. She snapped the rope that held her to the post, jumped over the side to the right and ran down an alley way. The flames had concealed her escape, just as she planned. She rubbed her wrists. The weakening of the rope by friction had worked, but still had hurt like heck.

She shook her head watching the crowd chant "Burn! Burn! Burn!" before bolting down the alley. A few moments later found herself outside of town in a wooded clearing. *This is perfect.* She began to run around the clearing in a clockwise direction faster and faster. The wind began to swirl pulling at the trees and their branches. Leaves and dirt followed in her wake. *They are going to see this soon. I must go faster.* Red increased her speed again, but then her legs balked slowing her. She hadn't yet recovered fully from the last jump.

"Faster!" she groaned. "I must go faster!" A crack of lighting hit in the center of the clearing and filled the area with the smell of ozone. A warp had formed.

Over the sounds of the storm she heard the distant shouts of an angry mob. They must have heard the warp opening and would be here any minute. She was tired. So very tired. "I must *jummmmmp!*" She shouted increasing her speed a bit more, silently praying it was enough. With a groan she ran for the center and jumped into the warp a second before the angry people of Salem reached the clearing. She felt herself being pulled between dimensions, between time itself and a second later she crashed out of the warp and landed onto a hard wooden floor with a thud.

"Ouch!" She exclaimed and rubbed her hip. "I really need to stop making such risky jumps." Red sighed, "Sure when people stop chasing me," and shook her head, "like that is ever going to happen." Red looked around the room she now found herself in. It was obviously a great deal later construction than the previous ones. A wooden door at the other end of the room lurched open and a large man stood in front of her dressed in an old-type business suit.

"Who are you? And how did you get into my house!" He said jabbing a finger into Red's face.

"Well, I sort of fell and well ..." But when Red tried to stand the pain in her hip caused her to wince.

Seeing her pain his tone softened. "You're hurt! Don't worry about it. My name is John Taration. I live alone and I don't use this room anyway, you can stay here if you like. It is not often I have a pretty lady in my company."

Red blushed. "Why thank you. I really appreciate the offer, but I wouldn't want to inconvenience you."

"No inconvenience at all. As I said I never use this room, or this house much for that matter. And what kind of man would I be to not offer a lady a place to stay? Especially one that has been injured?"

"Okay, you talked me into it. And John was it? I thank you, and I promise I won't stay long."

"Nonsense, you stay as long as you need. You won't bother me. I am a stock broker and often work late into the night. In fact, I will be leaving in a few days to travel back to New York City."

"Then what are you doing here? If I may ask?"

"You most certainly can," he said smiling. "This is my parents old house. They died a few years ago, now I use it for vacations. You wouldn't believe the stress the market can create."

Red laughed. "Oh I can imagine, quite well actually."

John ran forward and helped Red to her feet. "And what is your name pretty lady?"

"Red."

"Fitting. And fetching if I may say."

"You may." Red blushed and silently thanked God for the first person she met in a long time didn't want to kill her.

James shifted his position trying to get comfortable on the hard rock. "Sounds like he was a nice guy. Certainly better than the judge."

"What?" Red said as the question broke her of out her revere. "Oh yes he was. So much better. I wish I had met such a person at each jump. He didn't even ask me about my strange clothes!"

"Strange clothes?"

"Yes well keep in mind this was late 1800s and women didn't wear skin tight bodysuits. Heck no one did. Thankfully he was nice enough to let me borrow some of his late mothers items. I was not up to running for a while so, it was good to blend in."

"Wow late 1800s?"

"Yes, I had hoped to jump farther, but I didn't have the energy. But all things considered, I did very well to get that far."

"Well, any place would be better than where you were." James said with a smile.

"Don't be too sure. When being hunted by a Tyrannosaurus rex, even Salem during the witch trials looks pleasant!"

James laughed. "Yes I guess you are right. How long were you there?"

"Oh a few weeks. Possibly a few months. To be honest, I lost track of time during that jump. It had been quite a while since I was accepted and not actively being chased. It was a much slower time too than most. And I viewed it as a vacation of sorts. I could have jumped much sooner as my injury was a bruised hip. Not bad, but enough to prevent me from running at full speed and opening a decent warp for a few days."

"And he didn't mind?"

"Not at all. He left a few days after I arrived. Told me where to leave the key and to let his neighbor know when I left. Also, a nice man. The neighbor also hinted that John was lonely and could use a good woman like myself." She paused as a smile crossed her face. "He obviously didn't know me all that well. I was just glad no one recognized me."

"Recognized you? What do you mean?" James blinked and shifted again on his rock. The dirt floor of the cave was beginning to look better and better.

"Well, I was in the Salem witch trials, and I went ahead in time but not location. Therefore, I was still in Salem and being such a well-known event I was afraid that people might have recognized me. Thankfully, it was too early for photographs and after that much time ... people tend to forget anyway. It is amazing how quick we humans forget. I could tell you some amazing examples."

"Oh? Such as?" James asked intrigued.

"Well there was the time I jumped only 20 years ahead, and the family didn't recognize me at all. And they had called me one of their own!"

"Why did you jump?"

"Well that is a long story ... "

James looked out the front of the cave at the vast surreal landscape before them with dinosaurs grazing on tall grasses and the setting sun in the distance. "It would appear we have time."

Red laughed. "Time? A funny thing time is. Especially when you have been all over it like I have. But I digress. As usual I was being chased by someone. Well a group of someones. Okay, a mob. Pitchforks the works ... "

4

Red ran down the side street and ducked into an alleyway. They were getting closer. She should have never told him, it was foolish. You would think people of this time would be understanding. But oh no of course not. They want to kill the werido.

Red snorted. It would be her luck to end up in Geneva only a few years after Mary Shelley published *Frankenstein*. Apparently some people here thought it was a real account not a fictional tale and Red was one of the Victor Frankenstein's odd experiments gone wrong. Or at least the one boy she told (and showed how fast she could move her fingers) was scared enough to rally other people behind him.

Red tried door after door in the alley. All of them locked. She heard the mob getting closer. She had to find a way out or a door would be the least of her worries. Suddenly one of the doors she tried a few moments ago opened a crack. A little girl with darker skin than anyone she had seen thus far in Geneva looked out beyond the crack. "Yes?"

"Hello. My name is Red, could I please come in for a few moments? I don't mean to intrude, but, well, there is a large group of people after me."

The little girl looked Red up and down. "Why?"

"Because I am different."

The girl's eyes grew wide. "Ohhh. Come in." She said opening the door further. Red slipped inside just as the crowd reached the alley.

Red looked around the simple kitchen she now found herself in. "Thank you so much I–"

A fairly tall man with light hair and simple clothing appeared in the doorway leading out of the kitchen. "Lena! Who is this? Why did you–"

"Poppa! This lady was being chased," Lena said pointing towards Red.

"And you let her in? She could have done something very bad, and that is the reason they were after–"

"No. They chase her because she is different. They do that to us too. You said it is wrong and we should help those that are different."

The man's look of anger softened. "Yes I did my dear," his gaze shifted towards Red, "so someone was chasing you?"

Red nodded. "Yes. I have unique gifts. I made the mistake of showed a small boy while trying to befriend him. He then cried monster and the next thing I knew I was being chased by a crowd with torches and pitch forks."

"I see." The man said as he sat down at the small table in the kitchen. "Yes there are many in Geneva who have been frightened by the stories of galvanization and science gone wrong. Anything different they look at with great fear and contempt. Why they even judge us by the color of our skin!" The man said gesturing towards Lena and shaking his head.

"If you would like I can show you my gift. I think it might be best if you know what you are giving refuge."

The man raised his hand. "It is not necessary. I trust your face and my daughter is a good judge of character."

He then gestured towards the simple wooden table with two matching serviceable chairs that had seen better days.

Red walked over to the table, pulled out a chair and sat down as Lena made sure the door's bolts and locks were well secured. "If I may ask, why do you stay here if you don't feel welcome?"

The man sat back in his chair and poured himself a dark drink from the glass pitcher on the table, passed it to Red and poured himself more of the same. "A very good question. And don't worry the drink is apple cider, I have a friend that brings us some on occasion that is even safe for Lena. To be honest, I am a scientist and there wasn't very many possibilities in my country currently for a man of my vocation, so we came here. Unfortunately I had no idea the locals would be so hostile to anyone looking different from themselves. I spent all of our money getting here. Otherwise we would have left some time ago. Good jobs here are difficult when you look different. I had hoped the hysteria would have subsided by now."

"I see." Red said sipping the dark amber liquid in her glass. "Is there anything I can do?"

"Not unless you can get me a job or us out of here."

"Hmm. Let me get back to you on that," Red said thoughtfully.

"What can you do? You were the one seeking shelter."

"Well more than you know. But, how it helps us is the question. Yes I was, and I would like to repay your generosity."

The man raised his hand again. "No need. Your mere willingness to help is more than enough. It is more than anyone else has done for us." He paused and noticed Red eyeing them up and down. "You are wondering why my daughter is of a different color than I am?"

"No I–"

The man raised his hand again. "I can tell. It is quite all right, and I know you won't judge us. Lena, go check the door at the front is locked."

Lena blinked. "But Poppa I checked it a few minutes ago."

"Lena, please check it I want to make sure the crowd does not find Red."

Lena sighed, "Okay," then left the room.

The man made sure Lena was out of earshot and lowered his voice. "Red, what I am about to tell you, Lena must never know."

"Of course," she said nodding.

"My name is Georg Ohm. I was tutoring Lena's real father when he suddenly became ill. Everything possible was done but in the end he passed on. With his dying breath he asked me to take care of Lena as if she was my own. She didn't have any other family. I have kept my promise, and she does not know I am not her birth father."

Red leaned forward in her chair. "Don't you think she should know?"

"Of course, and I will tell her when she is a little older. She is such a tender girl and I don't wish to harm her in any way. I do think of her as my own daughter now, and would do anything for her." He sat back and sipped his drink just as Lena appeared in the doorway.

"The door is well locked Poppa." She said hopping into his lap.

"Thank you my dear." He said giving her a tender squeeze then poured some cider from the large pitcher. She smiled as she sipped it.

"You mentioned needing a job. I am guessing you are looking for a teaching position?"

"Yes. I would rather work on my research but that doesn't pay well," Ohm sighed.

"What research? Hmm, wait a minute, let me guess …electricity?"

Ohm blinked. "Why yes, how did you know?"

Red smiled. "Call it a hunch."

"A very good one." Ohm said still balancing his daughter on his lap.

"Another guess would be you would like to work on your research but you don't have the money for the materials you need."

"Sadly yes. My income has been very sporadic, never enough to continue my work or actually leave." Lena wobbled a bit uncomfortably then got down and pulled herself up into an adjacent chair next to her father.

Red thought for a moment. "What exactly do you need?"

"Well …" Ohm looked towards the ceiling in thought. "I have a theory I would like to prove, I have the details to build a new electrochemical cell that was recently invented. But I lack the money to purchase the components. If I could prove my theory, that should get me another position far from here."

"I see. And your theory has to do with the electricity, not the cell itself, correct?"

"Why yes. You seem very astute in your assumptions. Are you also a scientist?"

"No. Let's say I have a lot of insight. And you are just waiting for a stable power source? Yes?"

"Yes, that is the one missing part I need to test my theory." Ohm sat there even more intrigued by this young woman every minute.

"And how long would you need to prove or disprove your theory?"

"If I had a stable power source? Five minutes, perhaps ten. I would like to do the experiment several times, but even if I had one chance, it would help a great deal. Possibly even enough to secure the position I recently spoke of."

"Then I think I may have the help you need. I assume you have two large permanent magnets and copper wire?"

"Yes I do, but what–"

"And could I borrow a tall drinking glass? Oh and three pieces of short silverware? Perhaps forks?"

"Yes of course," Ohm said as he rummaged through several cupboards. "But what could you possibly do with these?" He said placing the tall drinking glass and several forks on the table beside Red.

"You shall see. First where is your equipment that you wish to use to prove your theory?"

Ohm pointed to the stairs behind Red. "Upstairs. I have made a small laboratory off of my bedroom."

"Perfect." Red said as a wide grin crossed her face then gestured towards the stairs. "Shall we?"

A moment later they found themselves in a small room. Originally designed as another bedroom, now converted into a small laboratory. Ohm handed Red the other items she requested and looked at her strangely. "I don't know what you think you can do with these items that can in any way, help me."

Red smiled again. "You will see. And what is that door to?" she said pointing.

Ohm shrugged. "The wash room."

"Perfect. Now will you connect these two wires to your equipment?"

"Of course, but what good–"

"Just keep an eye on your equipment and let me do the rest." She said closing the door to the wash room being careful to have the wire under the door, then got to work. She affixed the two large magnets on the outside of the glass and attached the wires. She then used another set of wire to carefully wrap the forks making them into a makeshift T apparatus completely covered in wire with each end equal distance from the other. Then attached them horizontally to the rod that Ohm had also provided. She then took the other rod and made a handle with it. She looked at the contraption and sighed. It was very crude but should work. If it would work well enough was the question.

"Are you ready?" She said through the closed door.

"Yes, although I don't know what good this will do."

"Don't worry about it. Just keep monitoring." She said sitting down on the chair which was the only furniture in the room. Red put the glass with its magnets on the outside between her knees and inserted the forks and rod into the glass. Holding the rod with the forks in one hand so they would stay in the proper position she grabbed the other rod and began to move it around and around in a circle. Faster and faster. She felt the wires warming slightly and knew it was working. At least somewhat.

Ohm suddenly shouted. "What!? How!? There is power! Keep it coming! I need more!"

Red spun the apparatus faster, then again increased its speed reaching beyond the metals normal tolerance. The heat began to build, and it had only been a minute. She wondered how much longer the makeshift generator would hold up. The center rod glowed brightly. "Hurry up!" Red shouted through the door. "I can't keep this up much longer!"

"Another minute!" Ohm shouted. "A few more seconds …there! I have it!"

Just then the generator's rod, coils and forks fell in on themselves into a molten mess in the bottom of the glass, smoking slightly. Red took off the magnets and opened the door handing Ohm the remains. "I am sorry, you might need a few more forks. And I doubt you will be able to use this glass again either."

"Forks? Who cares about mere forks! I have proven my theory! $I = V/R$! $I = V/R$! $I = V/R$! The distribution of electromotive force in an electrical circuit, and had established a definite relationship connecting resistance, electromotive force and current strength! I have proven it! I will need to do more research but with this data in hand I am sure I can get a better position and support for my experiments!"

Red smiled. "I am glad I could help a little."

"You have done far more than a little! And how did you do it?"

"Ah perhaps someday I will tell you. Right now I am very tired, could I rest for a bit?"

"Of course! Of course! My bed is at your disposal, it is the least I can do. Are you sure there isn't anything else I could do?"

"No. No thank you. The sofa I saw downstairs is fine. If you don't mind."

"Not at all. And yes by all means go rest. And thank you, if you ever need anything else, let me know."

Red collapsed on the sofa and instantly fell asleep. When she finally awoke it well into the night and both Ohm and Lena were fast asleep. She looked outside and finding the alleyway empty she slipped out locking the door behind her and ran for a forested area a little distance east of Geneva. A short time later she found what she needed. A secluded place to run at full speed. She started running clockwise direction. Faster and faster. A storm began to form, but no one was nearby to hear it . . . this time. With a crack of lightning, ozone filled the area as the warp formed. She continued to run. Faster and faster. The warp expanded, she ran for the center, jumped in, and disappeared.

5

"And you jumped ahead 20 years and Ohm didn't recognize you?"

"Correct. Neither did Lena. Of course, I didn't push them to remember. I simply located him and dropped by. I was in local period clothes by this time and he didn't recognize me at all. I suspect he would have if I had my usual bodysuit instead." She paused a moment to gesture at herself. "He did get that position he wanted and was doing quite well by then. But of course we know he did ... history tells us so," she said with a wink.

"Interesting, I would have remembered I think."

"Don't be too sure. We humans forget things very quickly in general. But yes some moments stay with us for our entire lives."

"By the way, I have been meaning to ask ... "

"Yes?"

James looked up and down the very curvaceous woman standing in front of him. "Why *do* you wear that bodysuit? Seems like different clothing would be less conspicuous?"

Red laughed. "Yes it would. But you see normal clothing is a large wind drag. The more aerodynamic I am, the less drag. Even a little variation in my speed and throw off a jump a great deal. I only once tried jumping without my bodysuit and it was not something I want to try again."

"What happened?"

Red tended the fire she built a short while ago then got up, walked to the cave entrance, and gazed into the night sky. "I was crazier in my earlier years and thought I could compensate. Boy was I wrong."

Red awoke in the street. *Where am I?* She gazed at the early morning sun peeking above the surrounding buildings. She remembered jumping again but nothing since. It was cold, not quite winter, but the air had a definite autumn feel to it. She pushed herself to her feet and looked around. The street was remarkably vacant. She walked trying to get her bearings looking up and down the empty streets. She finally came across a car in a 1950s style and knew she was somewhere in the United States. But where?

Red spied some clothes hanging on a line between buildings and sighed. She hated stealing, but didn't want a repeat of the previous jumps. Taking the dress, slip, and mid weight full-length coat she slipped them on and felt instantly warmer. Her feet continued to carry her down the paved road. By this time people started appearing on the side walk. Red jumped as a car horn nearby blasted her. "Hey get out of the road will you!" She turned seeing a man dressed in a business suit behind the wheel of his car. She nodded and got out of his way. "Try to be more careful! I would hate to see you hurt," he shouted driving past.

A few moments later she spied what she was looking for. A newspaper vending machine. Her vision blurred for a second and she shook her head to clear it. The effects of the last jump were fading, but still lingered. When the image finally resolved she read October 1st, 1957. "Hmm so I am in time," Red muttered to herself. She had long read about the first artificial satellite Sputnik and wondered what the reaction was by the common person at the time? Did people fear it as a form of attack? Or simply another aspect of the amazing times they lived in?

Red continued down the walk and started smelling the most wonderful scents wafting through the air. A few moments later her nose led her to the source, a small restaurant that was obviously getting ready for its breakfast customers. Her stomach talked loudly, and she realized that it would be a few days before the launch. Smiling she walked into the restaurant and spied the obvious owner. He was dressed in a suit with slicked black hair standing behind the counter, which did nothing to hide his large middle. "Hello, your food smells wonderful."

He smiled back. "Yes it does. Sometimes I don't think I should have gone into the restaurant business," he said patting his stomach. "Being here all day long isn't the best when you don't have any will power to resist," he chuckled. "Can I help you?"

"Yes I am new in town and had an accident. All my luggage and money were lost. I was wondering if I could work for you? I will work for some of that delicious food."

"Oh that is terrible. You will work for meals? Hmm." He said scratching his dark beard in thought. "Okay, you have a deal. I have a pile of dishes in the back that need washing. And you can sweep the floor back there, that would also be a big help."

"Thank you! And one last thing, you wouldn't happen to

have a place I could stay for a few days? Just until I can contact someone and get back on my feet?"

The man looked her up and down, having a little reservation after noticing the unusual shoes and bodysuit peeking out from under her skirt that didn't match the rest of her clothing, but quickly put it out of his mind. "Yes I do actually. There is a small storage room in back with a cot I use on occasion. But it is hard and I doubt you will want it."

"I am sure it will be fine for a couple of days. And thank you." She said heading into the kitchen to begin cleaning the mile-high pile of dishes, which she was sure was left over from the previous day. By the time she finished the breakfast crowd had already come and gone leaving another pile almost as large in their wake.

The cook, Silvia Hafpenny, laughed. "That is nothing, wait until you see the dinner dishes!" Silva was a large lady wearing an apron that had seen better days but still serviceable, already sporting several fresh stains from breakfast. She flipped on the ventilation fan to try to cool the warm kitchen. She left a few moments later heading off to the storage room to get more flour.

Red grumbled slightly cleaning the second batch of dishes, realizing that these people really did know how to make a mess of things. The owner poked his head in the kitchen. "Good job with the dishes. The cook mentioned how well they were done and she was relieved not to have to do them herself."

"Thank you. Glad I could help," Red said smiling.

"I told the cook you can have anything you like free of charge. Just ask her. You can eat in the back room as well, it is quiet and there is a small table."

"Thank you, I will."

"If you need anything else, let me know." He looked as though he was about to say something more but then the service bell went off. "Oh I have to get back, a customer wants something."

"Of course." Red nodded as the owner left the kitchen.

A few moments later Silva returned with her large bag of flour and placed it on the counter with a thud. "Whew, I don't know why they can't make flour sacks smaller. I know we go through it quickly, but they don't need to make the bags so heavy." She said opening the sack and filling several cups of flour to use in a biscuit recipe she was working on.

"Oh I am sure they will eventually," Red said smiling

Silva perked up. "You think so?"

"Oh I am sure," she said again still smiling, "I just wish they had dishwashers here now."

"What do you mean?" Silvia said a blank expression. "You are the dishwasher."

"I meant an automated device." Red said as she drained the dirty wash water and started to fill the sink again.

"Ohhh, yes that would be nice. But then you wouldn't have a job." Silvia said with a wink.

"True. But I am sure that there will be one soon."

"I have my doubts. The labor unions would have a fit."

"Trust me, they will come." Red smiled as she washed a particularly dirty plate being careful to rinse it thoroughly first.

Red and Silvia talked a lot during the day and her pleasant company really improved the otherwise menial and repetitive job. But one taste of Silvia's cooking, and she understood why so many people came to this restaurant. It was almost worth the entire days work. Silvia's cake was like a slice of heaven. Red never had anything quite like it before.

Red ate in the small back room. The table the owner had mentioned was tiny, but met her needs. The room's scratched and pecked wooden floors had seen better days and a slight dusty smell filled the air. Various information the owner wanted to keep at hand were tacked on the walls: bill dates, some IOUs, among other legal papers. She looked out the window at the late night sky. Everyone else had left, and the restaurant had long since closed for the day. Sitting back in the simple chair she ate the last piece of cake and sighed. Only a few more days of this and she would see what she came here to find.

Red slipped out of the dress she had worn for the day and into a night gown Silvia had provided. While a bit large, it would suffice. One of the problems with her gift was having to leave newly made friends so soon. Red sighed again, flipped off the light, and lay down on the hard cot.

A few days later all the newspaper headlines read the same: "First artificial satellite by Russia!", "Russians have beat USA into space!", or "United States falls behind the Russia!" The words may have varied, but the meaning was always the same.

"What do you mean she is a communist?" Silvia said looking at the owner aghast. "I think I would know if she was!"

"Well think of how she showed up? No clothes and the ones she had didn't match. I think she had Russian clothes on and when she showed up here had to change because our fashions are different. And her name 'Red' that is an obvious communist sympathizer name."

"I still think you are more full of beans than my chili! I have worked with Red very closely the past few days and I can tell you she is no communist!"

"Well the government will find out the truth," the owner sighed.

"You didn't!" Silvia shouted.

The owner nodded. "I did. The FBI will be here shortly."

"I have to tell Red!" She raced for the door.

The owner sighed. "I won't stop you, but I also didn't hear that or see you leave. Just make sure you are back here before the FBI arrive or they might take you too."

"Thank you," Silvia smiled, "I will be back soon."

Silvia left the restaurant and made for the old abandoned warehouse where she knew Red was likely to be. She had mentioned it several times as her place to get away from everything. It didn't take her long to locate Red on the second floor near a window watching the sun rise while writing in a book.

"Red!" She called out waving her hand as she ran over to her.

"Silvia? What are you doing here? We don't usually start for another two hours. Is there a problem?"

"I am afraid there is. The restaurant owner reported you as a communist sympathizer to the FBI." Silvia said trying to catch her breath.

"What? Why? What have I done?"

"Nothing and I tried to talk some sense into him, but he is afraid that if he does anything, they will call him a sympathizer as well. You know that Russian thing up there?" She pointed out the window towards the sky. "Has everyone frightened out of their wits. People are running scared and not thinking clearly. And apparently he is one of them. I know you are not a communist. And while I do have to admit you arrived a little differently, accidents can happen to anyone. It is no reason to report you as a Russian spy."

"Well I guess I won't go back to the restaurant."

"I am afraid it is worse than that. I am almost positive he told them of this place as well." Silvia said waving her arms around indicating the large empty building surrounding them.

"Dang. I need to get my things before–"

"You can't! I am certain they are there by now."

"Thank you Silvia for coming here and telling me. You had better get back to the restaurant, I don't want you mixed up in this mess as well."

"But what will you do?"

"I will think of something. Now go. I don't want you in trouble."

Silvia paused for a moment and hugged Red tightly. "Take care of yourself."

"I will. Now go!" Red smiled and watched her leave the building. A true friend and that was a rarity. She began contemplating how to get her bodysuit from the restaurant when several cars skidded to a stop in front of the building and men in suits jumped out of every door. "This can't be good," Red muttered.

The men pointed in several directions and began to encircle the building. It saddened her that the hysteria some historic accounts mentioned, were all too accurate here. She wondered how many other innocent people were arrested on such mentally lacking charges. She shook her head, now was not the time for such musings. The men were outside proceeding slowly, not knowing how many people were inside or their positions, but it wouldn't take them long. And she knew she couldn't get past them without being seen.

Red thought quickly. She didn't want to jump without her suit, but perhaps she could compensate for it. Hearing the men closing in, she decided there was little choice other than to try to jump here. Making her way carefully to the other side of the floor she closed the only door without a sound, and carefully lowered its wooden bar securing it. She knew this wouldn't keep them out for long, but hopefully long enough.

She hadn't tried jumping without her bodysuit as far back as she could remember. It was tricky enough opening a warp on the best of conditions. But could she do it wearing a dress with a full skirt? She kicked off the heels, thankfully the floor was clean except for a little dust. She lowered herself into the spiriting position and began to run in a counterclockwise direction. Faster and faster. But it was taking longer to reach her normal speed. A whirlwind formed but no warp. The extra drag was affecting her concentration as well as slowing her down. She pushed muttering "Come on . . . *open.*" Finally, there was a crack of thunder and the smell of ozone flooded the room. The warp was open. But it wasn't normal. It twisted in upon itself then back, the color fluctuating constantly between red, black, and green.

Red heard shouting and people banging on the door. Just as the door gave way it was ripped off its hinges by the whirlwind. She smiled and ran for the warp.

"Freeze!" Several men shouted but they were too late. For a second after they said it, Red entered the warp and disappeared from existence.

Red never felt her body pulled in so many directions before. This was not a normal jump. Below her waist felt like rubber and her tongue hung thick and slack in her mouth as though a hundred bricks were tied to it. She tried to direct the warp, trying to control it, but it refused. The universe spun. She gave one last try to stop this insane distortion and crashed out of the warp onto a wooden floor with a large thud.

Red woke not knowing how long she had been out and lay there wondering what happened and where or better yet when she was when she heard voices, apparently coming from below her.

"What the heck was that?" one man said.

"I don't know but Director Hoover is not going to be happy about this. Heck, he won't even believe us," said another.

"Okay let's get out of here and not say a word about this to anyone. They would likely lock us up!"

Red held absolutely still and heard several men say "Agreed" then footsteps heading off in the distance, cars starting, and tires squealing as they drove off. It was several minutes before she dared move. When she did finally get to her feet, she realized this was the same warehouse as before, just one floor up. Her head throbbed as though she had four migraines at once. She rested for a bit then made her way downstairs and found her shoes exactly where she left them.

The world shook and wobbled as she desperately tried to stay standing. Thankfully it passed after a few moments, but her headache continued, although less. She put her shoes back on, walked over to the window, and sat down wondering what to do next.

Then she heard Silva's voice call out. "Red? You here?"

"Silviiiia. Uppss heeere." She tried to speak but her rubber mouth complained.

A moment later Silvia spotted her by the window and ran over holding a suitcase. "You okay? I feared the worst when I saw all the cars here a bit ago."

"Yesss, willllllls beeeee inn aaa minute." Red said shaking her head to clear it. Whatever happened was finally dissipating. "I told you to go. I don't want to get you into trouble."

Silvia smiled. "Well I did, but then thought I would at least try to get your things to you." She said placing a suitcase beside Red. "I saw all the cars, so I stayed down the road out of sight, waiting until they had been gone for a while before I checked to see if you were still here."

Red smiled and hugged Silvia tightly. "Thank you my friend. This means more to me than you could possibly know. But you need to go. I do not want you to get mixed up in this mess."

"Well I doubt they will be back. They hopped out of here faster than a frog on a griddle. What did you do?"

"Nothing."

"Uh-huh. Well whatever you did it worked. I don't think they will be back to Altoona for some time," Silvia said smiling. "Are you sure you're okay?"

"Yes I will be fine. Best you get back to the restaurant, I don't want you to lose your job because of me."

"HA! Don't worry, he couldn't fire me even if he wanted to! He wouldn't know how to cook if God wrote it all down on the wall in front of him," Silvia said chuckling.

"You're probably right. Still, best you get back there. And thank you again for this," she said patting the suitcase.

"You are welcome. And why do I get the feeling I will never see you again?"

Red smiled. "You might, but probably not for a while. Now go my friend and please take care."

Silvia sighed and left the warehouse knowing she would likely never see Red again. But also realizing she had saved her life.

6

"So what exactly happened?" James asked as he added another log to the fire.

"Hmm? Oh you mean with the jump?"

"Yes!" James asked, a little irate at the question.

"Well, I am not exactly sure. What I do know is the clothing threw off my concentration and speed. Warps are not easy to open in the best of circumstances, let alone the worst. I apparently crashed out right before I jumped the first time. This means a paradox occurred: I was in same location at the exact same time. Thankfully, I didn't interact with myself or God forbid actually collided with the same warp I jumped into."

"What would happen if you had?"

Red rubbed her head at the thought. "Let's say that I had a bad enough headache with what happened as it was. I suspect that if I had appeared back at the same time of the first warp and collided with it, a temporal implosion would have happened. Beyond that I don't know. It could have destroyed the entire time-line, or just my own time-line. I hope that it would have been limited to me, but I don't know."

"Temporal implosion?" James blinked as he leaned forward.

"Well consider this, everything that ever happened on this planet never happened at all. In a mere moment all of time was eliminated. But that is the worst case. Hopefully, it would only have erased me from existence, not everyone. But like I said, I just don't know. And I have no intention of trying to find out one way or the other."

"I see. So it is very dangerous when you jump."

"Yes it is. But as long as I can keep my concentration, and speed constant there is no problem. Of course as I said opening a warp is still not easy in the best of circumstances, it just won't have the extreme situation I outlined. I really think it was due to my speed being thrown off by the air drag of the clothes, and that I jumped before the warp was ready. And believe me I won't do either of those again."

"I am sure. But what happens if you are separated from your bodysuit again?"

"Well now I carry a very form fitting backpack with a few essentials. And I always try to keep my suit with me in case I need it."

James looked around. "Where is your backpack?"

Red cleared her throat. "You took it!"

James grunted. "I did not!"

"Okay sorry, the other agents took it."

"Good thing you already had your suit on then."

"I am surprised you said that considering the situation." Red paused to gesture to the surrounding Jurassic land. "But yes I wasn't about to take that chance again. Besides in your time, bodysuits are not that unusual anyway." Red smiled and sat on a rock closer to the fire.

Gazing off in the distance deep in thought she finally looked back at James. "You really had no idea of what was going on did you?"

"I told you I didn't!"

"I know, but I have run into your type before."

"My type? What do you mean my type?!"

"Sorry, agents, FBI. They shoot first ask questions later. Or at least that is the ones I have met."

"Not all of us are like that. And I think the bureau is changing in that regard." James paused a moment and shrugged. "Sure there is still that element and some do go too far. Especially when national security is thought to be threatened."

"True but at least I know now where you stand."

"Where I stand? You only know now? I have told you several times–"

Red cut him off. "Yes you told me, but I have had people lie to me before. Sadly in my position is safer to assume the worst. But I am certain now because you didn't know about my backpack. If you were with the others, I could tell when it was mentioned. The others would have had a flash of knowledge in their eyes, you did not."

"I told you …" James stopped and hung his head then a few moment later raised it back up and looked into Red's eyes. "I thought you trusted me, after all we have been through so far."

"I do now. And I will prove it to you. The FBI does not have my real backpack, it is hidden away safe. In the same time-zone, but not in their hands. I couldn't risk them getting their hands on it and contaminating the time-line."

James eyes grew wide. "Contaminating the time-line? What is in it?"

"Well, a few items from the future which if released could severely damage the time-line. Of course the bag is protected, but I don't want to lose it all the same and need to retrieve it." Red said moving to rest her back along the cave's wall.

"Protected? How so?"

"It is constructed of a special fabric that can't be cut, torn or punctured. And if someone tries to open it without my DNA sequence, it will self-destruct."

"Self-destruct? You mean it will blow the building and anyone nearby?"

"Oh no, it won't harm anyone. It is far more advanced than that. It will simply dissolve."

"Dissolve?"

"Yes all the bonds that hold the molecules in place will release. The bag and all that is inside it will vanish. At most a layer of dust is left."

"Wow. And we come up with that?"

"Yes. But not for some time."

James looked out at the starlight night and heard a distant growl challenge that was answered by another farther away. He shuddered at the thought of large reptiles that saw him as a mere snack. "When can we leave this place?"

"Getting anxious?" Red asked while she poked the fire making sure it burned evenly.

"Very. I don't want to become a meal for one of those . . . things out there." He said jerking a thumb toward the cave entrance.

"Well neither do I. I think we can try tomorrow, but it won't be easy."

"Well you already said opening a warp is never easy."

"I know, but this is worse."

"Why do I get the feeling, I am not going to like this?"

"Perhaps because you won't. You see for some odd reason,

that I have yet to ascertain, dinosaurs are attracted to warps and the storms they create. It is almost like bees to honey."

"But you did it before, right?"

"Yes. But it took me several tries, and it was *still* close. Way too close."

"Hmm." James sat in thought, then got up, walked over to the cave entrance and looked out at the outline of the star lit grassy plain before them. "Would it help if I could hold off the dinosaurs?"

"With what? That little pea shooter you have?" Red chuckled. "That will only make them mad. It won't even slow them down in the slightest."

James turned with a smile on his face. "Well, it is not an ordinary 'pea shooter'. In fact, it is not a 'pea shooter' at all."

"Oh? It sure looks like it to me." Red said pointing to the gun in his underarm holster.

"Ah but it is far more. And to show you that I do trust you, I will tell its details. It is a new prototype I was allowed to test. Granted I am new to the bureau but with my top grades and background I was allowed. That and a good friend of mine is behind its development. I was heading to the test range when the alert sounded," he said sitting down again.

"What makes it so special?"

"Well first off it is not a projectile gun in the strict sense, but more of an energy weapon."

"Ahhhhh. Now that makes sense."

"Yes. It has the options for a pinpoint accuracy or one can widen the field for a large blast. Of course a large blast will really drain the energy reserve."

"Of course," Red said nodding. "Well how many shots can you fire before it needs to be recharged? And does it have a full charge now?"

James handed over the weapon to Red for her inspection. "It varies with the power of the shot. But yes, it does have a full charge. Push the status button on the grip and the grip will open with a screen giving its status, configuration, and programming options."

Red pushed the button and saw that the charge indicator did indicate 100%. She closed the door and handed it back to James. "Very nice. It might keep them at bay. But you will need to make every shot count as I am sure we only have one chance as we can't recharge it here."

"Actually, that is not an issue. It has the ability to self-recharge, which it does automatically when not in use. It takes a while to build up from zero but at least we don't have to worry about recharging it."

Red eyes lit up. "So *that's* where it went!"

"Where what went?"

Red threw her head back and laughed. "Sorry. You see, I have been to the future and there was this one-of-a-kind prototype of self recharging pistol that disappeared. Shortly after the disappearance, all the records, blueprints, and data also disappeared or were destroyed. No one knew what happened. It took a great many years before anything that even came close to it was developed. You have a very valuable piece of hardware there." Red said pointing to the gun now firmly holstered at James' side.

"Really? Wow. But …does that mean …something happens to me?"

"Why do you say that?"

"Well …if the gun disappeared and was never recovered …and since if I could I would return it …"

"Ohhhhh! I wouldn't worry about it. Understanding time is difficult and gives me a headache just thinking about it.

And I travel in it all the time!" Red laughed at the irony of her statement.

"I see. So it is possible I do return it?"

"Yes quite possible. I have been to many time-lines. Time is very flexible, contrary to popular belief. And I have helped time along quite often as you have heard. Anyway, don't worry about it. If need be, we will figure it out if and when that moment comes. For now, it will be light in a few hours. We should try to get some sleep."

"What? With all of those things running around out there?"

"Well the larger ones that would see us as a meal are too large to get inside. And the smaller ones that hunt at night usually like darkness, the fire should help keep them at bay, and they should have their meal by now anyway."

James nodded. "All right that makes sense. I will try, but doubt I will get much on this hard ground."

Red laughed. "Actually this is better than a lot of places I have had to sleep. Do try as I think we will need all the energy we can muster in the morning."

As they both put two more logs on the fire and settled in for a rough nights sleep, James silently prayed he wouldn't end up dinosaur dinner.

Sunlight streamed into the cave as it peeked over the mountain side. James awoke with a start sitting up and found Red already awake. "Didn't think you would sleep eh? Somehow I think you managed it," she said with a smirk.

"I must have been more tired than I thought." He said stretching and heard several pops from his complaining joints. Walking over to the entrance he gazed at the now familiar landscape then turned towards Red. "When shall we try the jump?"

"Not for a few hours. It will be easier then I think."

James sat down upon his familiar rock then decided that the dirt floor was softer when his backside complained loudly. "If I may ask, you said that you don't trust many due to something that happened. Would you mind telling me?"

She sighed and looked into the distance. "I suppose not. One of the first jumps I can remember is warping back to Wisconsin winter 1960."

"1960? Why then?"

"Well at the time I was working for what I thought was a covert government agency."

James' eyes went wide. "Oh really? How did you manage to get involved with them?"

"I am not really sure. Anyway, they sent me back then to 'right a terrible wrong that created a terrible tragedy in our history' as they put it. Sadly I was naive enough to believe them."

Red crashed out of the warp and landed with a thud on the light snow covered ground. She looked around, pulled out a thermal blanket from her pack, and wrapped herself in it. She felt near the target but couldn't tell if it was the right town or not. Then she saw the lake and knew she had the right location. This was Olin Park as planned, the curving road opposite the lake proved it. She found a building that was closed for the winter and let herself in.

It was cold, too cold. She quickly changed into some clothing she had brought for the period: a grey knit minidress, black thigh high boots, and a matching coat. She voiced her displeasure at the selection, due to the mission type, but was told quite firmly that these clothes would allow her to blend in. She placed her bodysuit and shoes into her bag and slung it over her shoulder.

A few moments later Red headed north along the road. The mission was simple enough: Plant several of the latest charges along a bridge and detonate them at the proper moment. Red was not told anything more than a 'terrible tragedy would be averted'. She finally reached the *Wonder Bar*, the first sign of the city. Activity surged inside. The large antique clock on the wall, showed she had time, providing this was the right day.

Red managed to find an empty table and sat down. A short time later a waitress approached. "What can I get you?"

"Oh some coffee and apple pie if you have it."

"We sure do, right out of the oven. I'll get you a slice in a minute." She walked over to take another order then disappeared behind a pair of swinging doors. She reappeared with a cup, pitcher, and a slice of pie. The waitress filled the cup with steaming black coffee as she sat a plate in front of Red. Wisps of warm vapor emanated from apple pie. "There you go. Anything else?"

"No, that is all thank you."

The waitress scribbled something on her pad and gave it to Red. "Give that to the lady over there by the bar to pay your bill."

"Thanks. Oh and do you have a copy of today's newspaper?"

"Sure. On the stand near the bar." She said pointing to a small table next to the bar that held all manner of newspapers and magazines.

"Thanks again."

"Welcome, have a great day." She said before walking off to other customers.

Red finished her pie and coffee then approached the cashier. She handed her the bill and paid with money the agency had given her. "Thank you, and I hope you come again." The cashier said as she operated the register.

Red walked over to the table and gazed at the array of papers. She smiled when she saw *"Madison Wisconsin Capital Times* Monday, October 24, 1960" at the top of one of the newspapers. For once she was in exactly the right place and the right time. As she turned to leave, several more of the lunch crowd arrived filling the establishment. She looked around thinking it was odd for so many to be here, for it was obvious they were woefully understaffed. If this was normal, they would have more waitresses. Red shrugged at the thought as she left, it was probably just a coincidence.

Red made her way north, found the bridge as planned, and got to work. In a secluded location she secured a rope and lowered herself down to get a look at the substructure. She smiled as she located the maintenance walkway and swung herself toward it. After several tries, she managed to grab hold and pull herself to one of the larger beams. Being careful to secure her line to the beam, she unhooked the hidden harness under her clothes and moved slowly on to the adjacent beam. Red silently cursed at the impractical clothing that the agency had insisted on in case she was seen, and inched her way across the beam. The wind pulled and pushed at her, threatening to throw her off balance. After what seemed like hours, she reached the walkway and crawled over the railing.

Red opened her bag and found the devices the agency had given her. She gave a sigh of relief when both the green status indicators lit up showing they had not been damaged in the jump or her mountaineering under the bridge. The devices were the latest in explosive technology. A hybrid of normal explosive, sonic disruption, and cloaking. The sonic aspect magnified the small chemical explosive charge one hundred times its normal disruptive capabilities. Then the cloaking technology made sure the device was not found once placed by blending perfectly to where it was attached.

Red checked her watch, then set each device for one hour time delay, placed one on each end of the maintenance walkway, and activated the cloaking system. Instantly the devices took on the same look as the beams she had attached them to and disappeared. Unless someone ran their hand across them and felt the bump in the structure, there was no way for them to be detected. After double-checking both devices, she hopped over the railing and inched her way back to the waiting rope. Then hauled herself back up.

Finding a place to hide and watch the explosion was not difficult. "A lot of traffic on this road today," Red muttered to herself. As the minutes clicked down a large group of vehicles approached. "Wonder what that is all about?" Her eyes went wide as a gasp tore from her lips. "Only a minute left. They can't be the real target can they? The agency said no one was on the bridge at the time!" When the group reached the halfway point, the charges detonated. Bright flames erupted from both ends of the bridge and spread along the superstructure severely weakening it. The bridge groaned as sections tore apart. The metal gave one last complaint of torture before everything and everyone fell down into the lake below.

"Who was on the bridge?" James asked excitedly.

"You wouldn't believe me if I told you."

"I am talking with a woman who can travel through time and you think I won't believe you?" James laughed. "Hardly!"

"John F. Kennedy or more popularly known as JFK."

James choked. "What? But we know he didn't die in 1960!"

"Well, yes."

"So it was a decoy or something?" James asked while pacing back and forth in the cave.

"No it was him."

"But how is that possible?"

"Because I altered time. I told you time is very flexible, much more than people like to think."

"Well yes, but JFK? What happened?" James blinked unable to believe his ears.

Red sighed and walked over the door of the cave and gazed out upon the field watching a couple of herbivores make short work of what humans would think of as large trees. "Nothing I am proud of. Basically I was fooled into believing the agency was telling me the truth. And they did not. I managed to get back to the time I left, only to find everything changed. The agency I knew of no longer existed. Actually, not much I knew existed anymore."

"You see, Kennedy pushed the space race into the race to the moon. Without him, that never happened. You can't imagine the number of technological advances that came out of the USA landing on the moon. Sadly other issues happened that compounded the situation setting technology back hundreds of years. Computers should have been artificially intelligent and the size of a thumbnail. Instead they were only the most basic machines still the size of buildings."

"Wow that far?"

"Yes. I am sure it was not the intent of the agency, but I never did find out their real goal."

"What did you do? Go back and talk yourself into not going ahead with the mission?"

"No. That would cause an extreme paradox, and God knows what would happen. I did go back though and after I saw myself place the devices, I disabled, and removed them. My first self was frustrated at the lack of explosion, but as I was doing everything 'by the book' I followed protocol and assumed that the devices failed and self-dissolved. Therefore I returned to report a failure in the mission."

"So you did stop yourself after all?"

"Of a fashion."

"But how do you remember what really happened since you changed your own time-line?"

Red rubbed her head. "I try not to think about that too hard. The best I can come up with is since I am a time traveler I am also outside of time's direct influences. But it may have been I got lucky. Anyway I make darn sure I don't cross my own time-line like that again."

"I agree. Far too risky," James said nodding.

"I was very glad I could get the time-line back the way it was so easily. I could have spent years fixing that mess otherwise."

"Years? Why years?"

"Well you see each choice has an action and reaction. Even small choices we make can have a big impact at certain critical points in a time-line. At other less critical points in the time-line you could let off the temporal equivalent of a nuclear bomb and nothing would change other than someone would have taken a different road to work. Or perhaps someone picked a different hair color than usual. Choices that in the end, *generally* don't make a difference in the time-line."

"Really? And how do you know when one is at a critical point?"

"Well sometimes it is obvious. In this case, removing John F. Kennedy from the time-line would have a great impact. One wouldn't know what the full effect would be unless they traveled into the future to see, but you can be certain a lot would change. Other situations are much more subdued and you don't see any effects until much later on."

"I see. It would seem that time travel is far more dangerous and involved than I could have imaged." James said as he stood up and put out the last of the fire by kicking some dirt into the still glowing embers.

Red turned and smiled. "Welcome to my world."

— 8 —

The sun was hot and high in the sky, shining down on the prehistoric world. James was already sweating, wanting to remove his suit jacket. But then thought better of it. He stumbled as they picked their way past the last line of the rocky outcropping that eventually, made up the cave system. "Finally, I am glad to be on the flat, I never did like mountaineering," James groaned.

"I wouldn't be too sure of that. Down here on the plain we are easy pickings for the larger animals. And believe me, most of them can run much faster than you."

"I bet, but I am sure they can't out run you."

"Generally no. But I hate to burn up energy running from them instead of warping out of here. Besides, I don't think I could go fast enough carrying you, if that is what you were thinking," Red said with a smirk.

James laughed. "No, not exactly. And I agree you don't want to waste the energy. Where shall we try it?"

"A short distance ahead should be a large enough area. With luck, we will be out of here before anything notices."

"And where you ever lucky like that before?"

"Er … ummmm … no."

James sighed. "You know, somehow that does not instill confidence."

"It wasn't suppose to," Red laughed. "You simply do not understand how difficult it is to open a warp."

"No, but I am beginning to."

They made their way to the center of the large plain. Not only did it give Red a lot of room to create the warp, but more importantly, it gave them a great vantage point. "All right, I will start slow. Is that gun ready?"

"Yes, I double-checked the status before we left the cave."

"Good. This may be a dumb question, but have you ever fired that thing before?"

"No. I told you that I was heading out to test it at the firing range."

Red sighed. "Great so it may not work at all."

"Oh it will work. I have no doubts about that."

"How can you be so sure?" she said stretching and warming up.

"Well Doctor Keleeigan, the friend I mentioned that designed this, had run many tests before I was permitted to use it."

Red's eyes flashed with momentary recognition. "Ah, I see. Well hopefully it works like it did in the tests!"

"I'm sure it will. And I'm ready when you are." James said pulling the gun out its holster and flipping off the safety lock.

"Okay." Red dug her foot into the dirt like a sprinter. "Let's do this!" The change in the air was immediate as it began to swirl kicking up dust, dirt and debris. Red increased her speed, and the storm grew in size and intensity.

Then they heard a beller. An ancient challenge from a world long since forgotten. A strong throaty sound that went right through and shook you to your very bones. "I think you had better hurry!" James shouted trying to be heard over the storm.

"I *am!*" Red shouted back.

A moment later a large Tyrannosaurus rex appeared on the edge of the clearing and began to race toward them. James raised the gun. The shot hit in the chest but the massive animal barely noticed. Red continued to run. With a thunderous crack a lightning bolt hit the ground and left a flickering diamond shaped hole of raw temporal energy in its wake. The warp fluctuated wildly between red, blue, and solid black. James raised the power level and shot. This time the energy beam was noticed, but not in the way he wanted.

"Oh shoot! Red! This is not working! *Hurry!*" James shouted as the animal's eyes glazed full of anger and vengeance as it ran straight for him.

"I am trying!" Red shouted back. "I am already getting tired, and the warp is not stable yet!" Red tried to run a little faster, but she felt it was useless. The added strain of trying to open a warp large enough for both of them, from so far back in the past was too much.

Then an Utahraptor appeared in the distance. A large one with at least a ton of muscle running fast towards them on its two legs. A moment later a pair of adult three ton Allosaurus also entered the clearing approaching fast.

"Reeed! Hurry!" James shouted but then realized that there was nothing more she could do. She was doing her best, and it was not enough. He sighed and quickly opened the gun's grip control center and put it on maximum power. He wasn't sure what would happen and Doc had told him never to try, it had not been tested. He flipped the window in the grip control closed, aimed, held his breath. The Tyrannosaurus was almost upon them, another second and they would be a meal.

James squeezed the trigger. The shrill blast rang in his ears. A cone of pure energy lashed out from the barrel and hit the Tyrannosaurus rex head-on. It stunned him for a moment. Then as he tried to move, each molecule came apart in a chain reaction, building exponentially, and microsecond later he disappeared into nothing.

"James! What did you doooooo?!?!" Red shouted in panic. James felt rather than saw her speed had increased. He turned his head just in time to hear a sonic boom. The warp had doubled in size, perhaps even tripled.

"I just! Red! The warp!" James pointed, hand trembling.

"James! Go! Now! I am fading!" Red shouted but James could see the warp had already decreased in size.

He wasted no time and jumped into the warp. Red was not even a millisecond behind him. Pulled through time and space, their senses were awash in color and light. Then after what seemed like an eternity, they crashed out landing with a thud.

James shook his head trying to clear his vision. After several minutes the ground resolved. "Wood?" he muttered. He got to his feet hearing sea gulls in the distance. Red was dazed and half asleep next to him laying on the wooden decking. Looking around James finally saw the ship they were on for what it was, with the large black pirate flag flying above his head there could be no mistake.

He grabbed Red. "Red! Red! We have to get out of here!"

"I...am...too...tired. Must...sleep..."

"You can sleep later, we need to get away, now! If you can't I will carry you."

"Hmmm? Okay..." She barely mumbled before falling sleep. James picked her up and started moving forward to try to get off the ship when suddenly, there was a lot of commotion from below. Including several loud voices.

A moment later several large men surrounded them wearing various types of clothing. Some were barefoot, others had well-made boots. It was obvious their look was by choice rather than something forced upon them. All of them held their swords drawn pointing at James making him feel as though he was in the middle of a deadly cage. One false move and they were done for.

All the men sneered at the two people in their midst and talked among themselves when they suddenly parted revealing a tall man with long black boots. The rest of his clothing was dark except for the brightly colored coat that looked to be made of silk. He had pistols on either side of his belt and a sword in its holster. He stroked his thick black beard. "Well well well. What have we here?"

"Who are you and where are we?" James asked but then quickly regretted the question.

"Who am I?" The tall man laughed which caused the other men to join in. After a few minutes he raised his hand for silence. "I am Edward Teach and you are aboard the *Queen Anne's Revenge!*"

"Blackbeard?" James said his eyes wide while looking the man up and down.

"No. You may call me Mr. Teach or as my men call me, Captain." The man began to stroke his thick bushy beard thoughtfully. "Blackbeard? Is that what they are calling me now? Hmm …I rather like it." Teach said drumming his fingers against his chest in deep thought.

"What shall we do with them Captain?" One of the men asked.

"Throw them over the side!" A man with a striped shirt shouted.

"Nah boil them in oil! That be best!" said another.

"No kill them now! Return them to the devils bosom! Everyone knows women are bad luck at sea and this one has red hair as to be of the devil!"

Blackbeard raised his hand. "That is for me to decide. Secure them below in one of the old slave cells!"

"Yes Sir!" They all shouted at once and led James, still carrying Red, below deck.

Down below James sat on the only thing available, the filthy cot attached to the iron bars. One of the pirates watched from his position through the bars. He could tell from the look in his eyes this pirate only held utter contempt for them and was part of the group that wished to throw Red, and himself, overboard.

He had tried to make Red as comfortable as possible. While they were given food, it was not something even a mouse would want. James thought it was probably best that she was still asleep. He could feel the ship had changed course, and the wind was carrying them at a faster speed. No doubt Blackbeard has something up his silk sleeve.

A good eight hours later Red finally stirred. "Where are we?" she said sleepily.

"The *Queen Anne's Revenge*. Beyond that I have no idea." James said gesturing to keep their voices low. The guard was still nearby though now fast asleep.

"The *Queen Anne's Revenge*? Are you kidding?"

"No, I wish I was. Do you know it?"

"Of a fashion. I warped out last time right under ole Blackbeard's nose. He didn't get a good look at me or what I did. Thankfully, it was one of the times I kept out of sight."

"Lucky for us then."

"Yes. Of course I don't know if that incident is his future or his past at this point. Either way, it shouldn't affect the time-line since he doesn't know anything," Red said with a smile. "And by the way, what the heck happened?"

"What do you mean?"

"With that last jump!" Red exclaimed in hushed tones. "I was fading from the strain of trying to open a warp large enough for us both that far in the past and the next thing I know, my energy and speed increased ten fold. I couldn't maintain it, but wow I never ran so fast before."

"I noticed."

"Well Mr. obvious, what the heck happened?"

"I'm not sure. The T. rex was almost upon us. The normal settings weren't having any effect. So, I dialed it up to maximum."

Red's eyes went wide then sat up on the cot. "Maximum? Are you serious? Why do I get the feeling that was dangerous?"

"Well ... because it was? I had no idea what would happen. Doc warned me never to try it."

"Then why did you?! You could have killed us!" Red said sharply.

"Shh keep your voice down, that guard is asleep and I don't really want him hearing us. Yes it could have. But so could the large dinosaur that was about to make a meal of us. You were fading ... losing speed, and I suspected you would haven't had enough to get away by then. I decided we didn't have anything to lose. I dialed it up to maximum and fired. The blast vaporized the T. rex, but I think it had an odd effect of giving you added speed. The warp opened wider, and we both jumped before it could contract."

"Hmm, well I certainly never had that happen before, and it would appear to have boosted my abilities as well as speed. We shouldn't be this far ahead in time. It should have taken us fifteen jumps or more to get here. Where is the gun now? I assume you kept it hid and were waiting until I recovered before making your escape?"

"Don't I wish. While I have been waiting for you to recover ... I ... well ... um ... don't have it," James sighed.

"What?! Where is it? How did you lose such a valuable piece of hardware?!" Red said utterly disgusted.

"I didn't lose it. Blackbeard's men took it. I couldn't drop you and go for the gun now could I? And in any case, I did think about if I used it, how much it would contaminate the time-line."

Red blinked. "What do you mean drop me? And you are right about contaminating the time-line. Imagine how history will change when he fires that gun!"

James smiled. "Well I had to carry you. You were in no condition to be led anywhere, and I wasn't about to let the pirates get their filthy hands on you. As for the gun, he won't be able to fire it."

"Why not? It is shaped similar to his black powder pistols. I think he can figure it out."

"Well true, if it didn't have the hand code enabled. Without my fingerprints to open the grip and punch in the code to tell it to disable the lock down, it won't do anything. I didn't know where we would end up on our next jump so I took the precaution of enabling the lockout code earlier."

Relief washed over Red, then dissipated almost as quick. "Oh great. So all we have to do is get out of here, get the gun, and jump again before they try to kill us. Simple," she snorted.

The large outer door to the slave cell area rattled and woke the guard. He jumped to his feet, a second before Blackbeard entered.

"Jon, the cook has an extra share of rum for you. You have earned it." Blackbeard said while he jerked a thumb over his shoulder. "I will watch these two."

"But Captain, they be from the devils bosom and full of trickery. We know they didn't arrive here from another ship. I don't think I should leave you alone with them."

"Jon I will be fine. I have my pistols, don't I? And they are locked up, what can they do?"

"True," Jon said nodding.

"And am I not Captain?" Blackbeard said with a smile. "Now go and enjoy your rum."

"Yes Sir." Jon said as he passed Blackbeard and headed up the steps. Blackbeard turned and secured the large heavy door after him. Then walked over and glared at the two prisoners on the other side of the bars.

"Now then, who are you and what are you doing on my ship?"

"What difference will it make? You will kill us anyway," James said. "We know how you are! How are we to die? Drawn and quartered? Keelhauled? Sword through the heart and our heads hung from the sails?"

Blackbeard threw his head back in a large laugh as he pulled over a medium-sized barrel, stepped over it, then sat down. "Nothing of the kind!"

"But we know–"

"My dear Sir, that is what I *want* people to believe. A fearful reputation is worth far more than ten ships like this for a man in my position. But I am hardly the person my reputation leads them to believe. I haven't corrected them as it is to my advantage."

"Then you are going to let us go?" Red said trying to give her best smile.

"At the proper time. I can't appear weak in front of my men." Blackbeard said leaning forward placing one hand on his knee. "Now shall we start this again? Who are you and what are you doing on my ship?"

"Well–" Red began but James cut her off.

"We are travelers. We came upon your ship by accident. We are not against you or your crew." James said trying to sound convincing.

"So you are travelers, eh? Then why didn't I see any ship around when you arrived? Answer me that one!"

"We–"

Red leaned over closer to James. "James he knows."

James turned toward her. "Knows what?"

Blackbeard laughed again. "My dear Red, you thought I didn't notice you before? You should learn that nothing happens on a Captain's ship without his knowledge of it. But do not worry, your secret is safe with me and no one else knows. Or will know."

"Thank you." Red said with great relief in her voice.

"We are under full sail at the moment. At some point I will *arrange* for you to escape, be ready for it. You can then disappear again." Blackbeard said as he stroked his thick beard. "Is that acceptable to you both?"

"Oh yes of course! That will be fine. But if I may ask ..." James said.

"Yessss?"

"One of your men took an odd pistol from me, can I have it back?"

"Oh that thing? I don't see why not. It was a gift from someone I suspect as it certainly is not functional. I couldn't even find a place to put the powder in!" He laughed then looked back at James. "You will have to *steal* it. I can't be seen giving it to you. Understand?"

James nodded. "I understand."

"Most of the crew thinks it is solid silver, although I know silver and that not be it. By the way, do you know who cleans my bedroom?"

James blinked. "Umm ... no."

"A mermaid," Blackbeard said slapping his knee. "Sorry, but I have been wanting to try that out for a long time.

Overheard it from one of my crew. Of course, I can't tell it to anyone here, it would damage my reputation," he said with a grin.

Blackbeard got to his feet. "That pistol is in my cabin, in the desk, second drawer on the right. I will leave the door unlocked at the appropriate time. But make sure no one sees you take it." He shoved the barrel over to its original position with his foot right as the door behind him swung open.

"Thank you Captain. That be good rum," Jon said.

Blackbeard nodded. "As you can see nothing happened here. Be sure to keep a close eye on them though." He said as he turned to leave.

"I will Captain, have no fear."

"See you do. Or it will be your hide." Blackbeard said over his shoulder then shut the door behind him.

A short while later the rum had done its work and Jon was sound asleep leaning against the bars. "What do you think?" James whispered. "Do you think we can really trust him?"

"I don't see that we have a choice. And I had no idea that he spotted me. He must have right as I jumped. I know there was not anyone else around then. He is more intelligent than anyone gave him credit for," Red whispered back.

"When do you think 'the proper time' is?"

"I am not sure. I think we will know though."

"I hope so. Where, er when, where you here before?"

"During the time he held Charleston hostage with a blockade. Unfortunately his men got side tracked in town when delivering the ransom. As he didn't really want to kill anyone, he came to investigate. I helped get the ransom together and delivered it as he arrived. I disappeared undetected right after that. Or so I thought."

"Ransom? You helped the pirates steal gold?"

Red laughed. "No I wouldn't have helped them with that. They wanted medicines. I never did find out why, but I figured ol' Blackbeard must have had a good reason. While I helped with the situation, there is no mention of a woman with red hair in the accounts of the deal. Probably because Blackbeard kept that part quiet. Like I said, he is more intelligent than people gave him credit for."

James sat with his eyes wide. He had heard many stories of Red's exploits but every one seems more amazing than the last. "Hard to believe that pirates would want medicines instead of gold. History only mentions gold and greed."

"Well the accounts are rather obscure. Not to mention Hollywood has changed the pirate look in so many ways, most people don't know the difference between fact and fiction." Red leaned back on the cot, resting her back against the bars. "I think we are heading north since the land is on the port side."

"How can you tell?"

"Well you see since Blackbeard remembers me it must be after Charleston. And he only sailed north of there after that so obviously we are off of the east coast." Red paused to point to the small tiny window above them. "And we can see the land on that side of the ship."

"So elementary my dear Watson?"

Red laughed quietly. "Exactly. He should put in port somewhere for supplies soon. They didn't carry much at any given time. Water went bad quite quickly for example. Of course, I doubt these guys drink much water," she said stifling a chuckle.

A few days later, just as Red thought, *Queen Anne's Revenge* anchored off some remote island and most of the crew went ashore for supplies. Jon was asleep, as usual, sitting on his barrel and leaning on the bars. His snores seemed louder than normal. Red carefully lifted his keys, and without a sound, unlocked the door. Motioning to James, they quietly crept past the sleeping pirate and left the cell area.

James quietly closed the door and turned to whisper to Red. "You go get a launch so we can go ashore and I will get the gun from Blackbeard's quarters."

Red raised an eyebrow. "Are you sure you can find it?"

"Yes, shouldn't be a problem, he told me right where it is after all. You be ready to leave. I want to be off of this ship as soon as possible."

"You and me both. Good luck." Red said as they both separated.

James climbed up a deck and went aft. He picked his way through various storage areas then up another deck and came upon a large wooden door with the words Captain embossed into the wood. Carefully opening the door he found the room uninhabited as he expected. He located the desk on the other side and pulled on the second drawer. But it stubbornly it refused to open. There wasn't a keyhole so there must be some other way it locked.

Looking carefully at the desk, he smiled as a thought flashed into his mind. Pulling out the first drawer an inch and the bottom drawer three inches he heard a soft click. Sure enough, the drawer was now unlatched and slid open easily. Inside he found his gun and a note laying on top of it.

"I knew you would figure out how to open the desk. And shows how much smarter you are than the rest of my crew. Make sure you are gone before I return or I will have to kill you. Also make sure I never see either of you again.

Edward Teach, now known as Blackbeard."

James stuffed the note into his pocket and flipped open the

gun's control panel. It had fully recharged and was ready to use. He dialed back the power setting, closed the control panel, and looked up in time to see cabin door swing open revealing a large wide-eyed pirate standing in the doorway.

"How did you get in here?! I'm going to–" but the man never finished the sentence as James fired a silent stun blast. The man was unconscious before he hit the deck.

"Careless of me." He muttered, then dragged the man inside the cabin. After tying and gagging the man in Blackbeard's sheets he made his way up to the top deck.

Red was getting anxious. It had been over fifteen minutes, James should have been able to get that gun by now. She had a launch ready, but a feeling that the rest of the crew would be back any minute nagged at her. "Where is he?" She breathed as one of the doors leading below decks swung open and Red's heart leapt into her throat.

"James!" she said in a hushed tone. "What took you so dang long?"

He looked around, then helped her into the launch. "Our Blackbeard has a unique sense of humor."

"What do you mean?"

"Oh he told me where the gun was all right. But not that the drawer in question had a trick way to open it."

Red chuckled. "Yes, he does have a sense of humor, but rarely shows it."

They slowly lowered themselves to the water and rowed to shore. Thankfully, they found a beach separate from where the others had landed and worked their way along a small stream. Soon they came upon a clearing near the tallest point on the island. "Will this work?" James asked pointing to the large area in front of them.

"Yes it should. Are you ready?"

"As ready as I ever will be."

"Okay. Let's do this!" Red said as she began running and the air begin to swirl. As she increased her speed the soft sandy soil also became airborne. It was like being in a whirlwind of sand, dirt and debris. Half a minute later there was a crack of thunder as a lightning bolt shot to the center. In its wake a rip in space and time had formed and rapidly grew in size.

"Red! The warp! It is open! Now?"

"Yessssss …noooww!" She shouted but James already knew she was fading fast. Another moment and it might be too late. He ran and dove head first into the warp with Red right behind him, a second before it slammed shut.

$$-\,10\,-$$

The air swirled as a bolt of pure energy stuck and a red rip into the fabric of space and time opened in its wake. A moment later James fell out onto an iron plated deck with Red landing a second later right on top of him. The warp closed behind them leaving no trace as usual.

"We really need to stop meeting like this." James said giving Red a squeeze.

"Will you cut it out! Now where are–" A incredible bang ripped through their ears and they smelled old-fashioned gunpowder, as a cannon shell whizzed over their heads. "Holy! They are shooting at us!"

"Not us! That other boat over there!" James pointed towards the unusual ship. Most of it was pyramid shaped, very little else could be seen except for the large anti-ship guns sticking out at different angles and the large smokestack in the center. Then another explosion as the other ship fired a shell. It whizzed over top of them and bounced off the metal-covered turret right behind. They covered their ears against the extreme audio assault.

"Where the heck are we?" James shouted still trying to keep his ears covered. "You landed us in the middle of a war zone!"

"I did not! You know how tricky–" Red shouted back, but didn't dare uncover her ears.

"Well you are the one driving!" James shouted as another shell went wild and bounced off the decking nearby. They both were very grateful the shell did not explode or it would have killed them instantly.

"Well my driving has got a lot worse since you tagged along!"

"What kind of ships are these?" He said pointing with his elbow to the unusual craft they were on. "I don't recall seeing these before. There isn't anything to this ship above the water line other than a gun turret and a smokestack! It certainly isn't a submarine." He said as they uncovered their ears.

"Oh my Lord …do you see the flag on the other ship?" Red said pointing. "It is confederate! We have landed in the middle of the Civil war! That has to be the *CSS Virginia!* I can't think of any other confederate ships that looked like that."

"*CSS Virginia?*" James blinked looking lost.

"Haven't you ever heard of the Battle of Hampton roads? The *Monitor* and the *Merrimack?*"

"The *Monitor?* You mean this is the first battle of the ironclads?" James said looking around. Images finally resolved in his mind, images from his old grade school textbooks. They must be on the *Monitor,* one of the most innovative ships ever built. He thought back to how the whole ship was put together in less than one hundred days due to all the parts being ordered and built elsewhere to exact precision. Then delivered and assembled. It was the first example of modular design and was never quite repeated the same way again. "Somehow they looked different in the old photos."

Another shell whizzed over their head causing them to hold their ears again and hug the deck. "Yes, the *Monitor!* And they probably look different because they are shooting at us! If we stay here, we are dead for sure!" Red exclaimed.

Inside the large gun turret one of the men saw something odd as the turret swung around to aim. "Sir, I could have sworn I saw people outside!"

"Well I am sure they are just watching the show, don't let up firing. Make sure you get that next shell rammed home properly or *you* can explain it to the captain why his gun didn't fire." Sam Greene said pointing to the muzzle end of the large gun.

"But Sir! I see a woman and a man out there!" The sailor said pointing.

"Don't worry about it, I have seen a lot of men and women. Do not slow down. Hey, get that primer in place!" He shouted pointing at the large object to his left. "What is so special about these two anyway?"

"They are on our deck sir."

"WHAT?!" Greene exclaimed. "Get your pistols and follow me. We need to make this quick!"

"I was fascinated by this ship," James said. "If I remember right behind the turret on the other side in line with the pilot house should be a hatch, we can use to get inside."

Another shot whizzed past and with a loud bang that reverberated through the decking as it bounced off the heavy iron plating of the turret. "And how are we suppose to get around and that far across the deck without getting killed Mr. *Monitor* expert? Hmm?"

"Don't move! I don't know how you got aboard but you are leaving now." Red and James both turned around to see three men pointing pistols at them. The one that had spoken wore officer's stripes, the other two were clearly enlisted men. Both were shirtless and sweating profusely.

"See Sir, I told you I saw two people through the gun port." One of the shirtless men said.

"You did indeed." The officer said then looked at Red then James. "I am Sam Greene Executive Officer of the *Monitor* and you will get off of this ship the same way you came or we will shoot."

"Get off how?" James said gesturing around them. "There isn't a boat around." A wild shot landed thirty meters away in the river with a mighty splash.

"We are not confederate, and would appreciate it if you would take us inside? It is a bit dangerous out here." Red gave the most convincing smile she could muster. "Please?"

"Well you are right, there are not any boats around and the captain might want to question you. All right move forward and don't try anything unusual or we will fire."

"Move to where?" James asked.

"There is an open hatch alongside the turret. Now move!" Greene said waving his pistol in the direction of the turret.

Red raised her hands. "We're going! We're going!"

A few moments later they were safely behind the *Monitor's* thick iron armor. They blinked in the extremely dim light trying to see. The air was hot and thick with the smell of gun powder and the stench of sweaty men. It was easily over ninety degrees, James and Red already began to glisten with sweat.

"Why do you have the lights turned off?" James blinked trying to see.

"The lights are on. You will get use to it." Greene said while he paused to use an old tube intercom. "Captain Worden, we have some prisoners here."

"Prisoners?! Where did they come from?" The Captain's voice came through the metal tube.

"I don't know Sir. Would you like to see them?"

"Not now, secure them in irons then lock them in one of the storage rooms. We will take care of them later."

Red and James were quickly secured in iron chains by two large sailors and locked into a storage room. All the while the guns were going off incessantly. Shells launched by the Merrimack were bouncing off the *Monitor's* armor causing the ship to vibrate over and over again with each hit. They could hear the Captain and Greene shouting into the voice tubes.

"They're going to board us, put in a round of canister!" The Captain said.

"Can't do it," said Greene, "both guns have solid shot."

"Give them to her then!" The Captain ordered.

Red and James heard one gun go off a moment later. But not two. "Wonder why not both?" James said.

"Shhhh," Red said, "we can't hear if you talk."

"Why don't you fire?" The Captain shouted.

"Can't do it, the cartridge is not rammed home."

"Depress the gun & let the shot roll overboard."

"It won't do it," Greene replied.

"How long will it take to get the shot out of that gun?" The Captain inquired.

"Can't tell, perhaps 15 minutes."

Red listened carefully and could feel the ship turning away in another direction. "They are moving off. Probably until they can get both guns working again."

James leaned against one of the closet's small walls and slid down to the floor. Looking around, he didn't see anything except food stored in metal cans and lavish plates with the name *Monitor* embossed in gold. Nothing he could use to open the cuffs. "Figures they wouldn't store the silverware with the plates." James muttered under his breath. He felt the gun under the jacket, but with his hands secured tightly behind him, he couldn't reach it. "Now what do we do?" he said looking towards Red.

"We wait for a moment we can slip away."

James eyes widened. "How?"

"Well I have an idea."

"Care to share? And if you are thinking of blasting the shackles with the gun, don't bother. I would have to configure the power level or we will blast a hole in the hull, not to mention us. And I can't do that with my hands behind me."

"I wasn't planning on using it, I don't want to contaminate the time-line by blasting our way out of here. I have another idea."

"Oh?"

"A little trick I learned about iron handcuffs on one of my jumps." Red smiled as another shot rang out. "Sounds like they fixed the guns."

"A splendid shot, you raked them then." The Captain said over the voice tube. "Look out now they're going to run us down, give them both guns." A moment later they heard a loud blast or explosion a short distance away.

"Well where was that Mr. *Monitor* expert?" Red said looking at James.

"I am not an expert, I was just interested in it." James said then thought for a moment. "Hmm, I think that was the pilothouse. It is really the only thing they can hit head-on other than the turret. I can't see how they could damage it through with the thick armor that is all over this boat."

"Gentlemen I leave it with you, do what you think best. I

cannot see, but do not mind me. Save the *Minnesota* if you can." The Captains voice came over the voice tube.

Reds eyes flashed. "I remember the Captain was badly injured near the end of the battle. Must have happened with that last shot. This might be our chance."

"How is that going to help us?" James said but Red quickly gestured for quiet. A moment later they saw Greene through the slots of the closet door. He was moving quickly towards the pilothouse. A few minutes after he had walked past, James risked speaking. "Looks like Greene is taking command."

"Yes. Be ready to move." Red said as another shot rang out.

"Move? How? If you didn't notice we are chained and inside a small locked closet."

"Oh ye of little faith." She said raising up her arms devoid of any restraints.

"You got them off? How?"

"I told you a little trick I learned. Now be quiet I think I heard Greene give the cease fire. The *Merrimack* must be moving off. This is our chance."

"If you haven't noticed I am a little tied up."

"Oh that little detail." Red chuckled as she placed her hands on the restraints. James felt a little vibration, and they popped open. "There you are. Now get that gun configured in case we need it. The lowest setting. And remember I don't want to contaminate the time-line. No one can see you use it."

"Of course," James nodded flipping open the gun's hidden control panel, "I don't want to change history either."

Red again gestured for quiet as she heard hatches opening. A moment later several men walked past their closet door and then it was all quiet again. Placing her hand against the keyhole plate she closed her eyes in concentration. After a few seconds James heard a barely audible click. Red smiled and opened the door.

"I don't know how or where you learned that, but I'm grateful," James whispered.

Red's grin widened. "Houdini actually. Nice guy. How do you think he got his name as the world's greatest escape artist?"

James' eyes shot open in surprise. "Houdini? Really?"

"Yes. Too bad this trick doesn't work on the newer locks. And perhaps sometime I will introduce you. Now let's go." Red said gesturing down the corridor.

They moved quickly but carefully aft. They didn't see any crew along the way and finally reached a small hatchway right behind the turret. Climbing its ladder they could just make out the crew through all the smoke talking on the other side of the ship.

"Perfect. As I thought, some of the spectators are congratulating them." Red whispered then pointed to a small launch sitting alongside the *Monitor* a few feet from them. The air was thick with smoke that stung their eyes and throat. "All this smoke will cover our escape. On my mark we make a break for it. Okay?"

James nodded crouching down, preparing to spring out of the hatch. "I'm ready."

"Now!" Red breathed.

They popped out of the hatch and sprinted for the launch, all the while fighting not to cough in the thick smoke. James jumped in and started rowing with Red helping a second later. The launch slid through the glassy water with ease as they made their way towards a dock they could barely make out in the distance. James could not hold back the burning in this throat any longer and coughed. But by this time they were out of range.

"I wonder if we are now in the history books?" James said as he coughed again.

Red hacked several times trying to clear her lungs. "I doubt it."

"Why not?"

"Well would you want to admit that two people showed up on your boat and then disappeared?"

"I suppose not."

"You know, I bet that is why Greene didn't make command of the *Monitor* other than the end of this one battle."

James laughed. "You're probably right."

‑ 11 ‑

The side street between two large brick buildings was quiet as a tomb. The moon shown down brightly as the air began to swirl kicking up dust and debris from the unpaved street. Suddenly there was a crack of thunder and a lightning bolt shot to the middle of the street cracking open a rip in the very fabric of space and time. The rip grew in size becoming fiery red then blue then red again as it expanded. James crashed through the rip landing face down into the dirt. A second later Red landed on top of him and the warp closed again a microsecond after.

"Ugh." James said spitting dirt, but thankful they didn't land three feet north into the pile of horse dung. "I wish one of these days we would land with our feet on the ground."

"Well, I am sorry. I never did invite you along you know." Red said as she climbed off of James and stood up.

"And I didn't join willfully either. Now where are we? That warp didn't feel like the others. Much too short. Felt like something was wrong?" James said as he stood up and brushed himself off.

"There was."

James stood there for a moment waiting. Then he looked directly into her blue eyes. "Well?"

Red looked down and sighed. "You know I didn't have enough energy built up to do a full jump. But you also know there was too many people around and we couldn't stay there. I figured I had just enough energy to jump some distance away. It is the time jumps that really drain me."

"So we are at the same time but different location?"

Red shrugged. "Approximately. It can vary a bit." Red said looking at the large brick buildings on either side of the dead-end alley. "Judging by these buildings and the dirt road," her nose wrinkled at the scents wafting through the air, "not to mention the horse fertilizer over there, I think we are probably near the same time. And in any case I didn't have the energy to jump far so we couldn't have drifted much."

"Well at least I doubt people here will be looking for us. But we should probably get moving in case the time storm attracted any attention."

Red nodded as they walked out of the alleyway and onto the dirt main street. The air felt hot and muggy, even this late at night. Mosquitoes buzzed. Trash lined both sides of the street. "This city is quite dirty and the sanitation really needs work," Red muttered.

"No kidding." James said as they turned a corner. This street seemed better than the last. Gas lamps dimly illuminated the street and surrounding buildings. Gazing off into the distance James eyes widened. "I think I know where we are," he said pointing. "Isn't that the White House several blocks down?"

It was now Red's turn for shock. "I think you are right. Wow, I didn't realize Washington was ever quite this dirty."

"Yes it would seem that we clean up well," James said chuckling.

"Funny, very funny. Well Mr. Comedian, I think we had

better find a hotel for the night. Wandering the streets in the middle of the night during a war could get us into trouble. And I think we have had enough of that lately, don't you?"

"Yes agreed. I think I see a sign at the end of this street. And the building looks better than the others we have passed."

Red nodded in agreement and they soon found themselves in front of a freshly painted sign saying *The Willard*. "But how are we going to pay for it?" James asked as he pointed to the elegant front doors beyond the sign. "We don't exactly have 1800s money."

Red smiled. "No, but I have an idea. Follow me and play along."

They pulled open the lavish doors and walked into the large reception area. Mosaic tiles covered the floor in the center creating a large 'W' in cursive, with well-made red carpets covering the floor where the tiles did not. Large detailed columns with ornate hand carved fixtures at the top and bottom framed the whole lounge and reception area. The ceiling was inlaid with mahogany wood in a square pattern. In the center of each square was a circular area in the middle with almost a star shape. The whole place radiated of money. This was the Washington they knew, and could tell it was where its current inception started.

Even with all the elegance, the air was even more oppressive inside than out. Hot, humid, stagnant air filled the room. A lady sat behind the large marble desk near the front. "This looks more like a mansion than a hotel," James whispered.

"Shhh and follow me." Red said as she walked up to the desk. Behind it the older lady continued reading a book, not noticing their approach. She was short with a white blouse and a dark skirt. Her hair was obviously very dark at one time, but now streaked with grey lightning it a great deal. After several minutes of them staring at her, she finally looked up.

"Well! Sorry I was in a good spot and didn't hear you come in. What can I do for you?" She said gazing at the large grandfather clock alongside the wall on her right then looking up and down at Red's unusual attire.

"We would like a room." Red said with her best smile.

"Oh? Rather late to be checking in. You are lucky I got reading my book and lost all track of time, or the lobby would have been locked. What are you doing out so late?"

"I guess we are lucky you are still here then. We just got in town."

"Just now? Why were you traveling so late? That can be dangerous, hard to see where you are going."

"Yes, but I have a relative here in town that is expecting us. We planned to arrive hours ago. But as you pointed out it is late, and I didn't want to wake her. I saw your lobby lights on and thought we might get a room here instead." James stood behind Red nodding in agreement.

"I see. Well you are indeed lucky as there are only two other people staying with us at the moment. Any particular room you would like?"

"Anything will do. We only need a bed for the night."

"All right. If you will sign the book here," the grey-haired receptionist said as she spun a large book around with 'Register' clearly embossed on the front cover in gold and opened it for Red, "you can have suite 5. It is down the hall, and here is the key." She pointed towards the room, then dropped the key in Red's hand. "I can call someone to help you with your luggage."

"That is not necessary. We don't have any," James said smiling.

The lady cocked an eyebrow at Red then James. "I don't know what kind of place you think we are, but we only have respectable people here. I think you had better leave now." She held out her hand for the key.

Red looked at her confused for a few minutes then her eyes widened at the realization then shook her head. "Ohhhh it is not anything like that. Someone stole our luggage on our way here. It is why we are so late."

"Oh you poor dear. You did have a bad day. And explains your attire. I assume whoever it was took your fine dress leaving you only in your underclothes?"

Red nodded again. "Yes. Apparently they didn't like James' clothes. You wouldn't happen to have something we could wear do you?"

"Yes I do. And I think the porter might have something for the gentleman."

"Thank you. It would be a great help," James said.

"Well I am sure you want to turn in for the night. Make sure you open a window to let the air circulate and use the mosquito net. This time of year they are bad," the receptionist said.

"We will, thank you for the suggestion. One more thing though."

She had already looked back down at her book but looked back up at red gazing over the rims of her reading glasses. "Yes?"

"Our money was stolen with our luggage."

"Oh I see. Hmm, well don't worry about that now. You both have an honest look about you, we will settle that later. Perhaps your relative can help you out."

"Thank you very much for your understanding. Yes we will take care of it don't worry." Red said grabbing James hand and headed off down the hall. They walked past several doors finally finding suite 5 at the end. Using the key Red unlocked the door, pulled James inside, and locked it behind them. Red reached for the gas lamp and turned the valve. The room brightened, and they stood in shock. The room was semi-circular and had several sections. The walls were white, and each section was lavishly decorated with well padded upholstered furniture. The bedroom was off to the side. The center room held a large fireplace. On the other side was a restroom. Over the bed a mosquito net had already been placed.

"And how are we going to handle paying for this?" James whispered. "We won't be any better off tomorrow than today."

"I know, but we will think of something." Red said still looking around the ornate room. The air was indeed stuffy, and she quickly opened the several windows to let the weak breeze try to clear it.

"Like what?" James said taking off his coat and laying it over a rosewood chair with a red cushion. His shirt was soaked with sweat especially under the arms. He had wanted to remove it earlier but didn't dare expose the gun to those who might be walking by. He took off the holster and hid it under his jacket while taking off his shirt.

"I don't know, we will think of something," Red said sitting on the bed. "At least the bed is comfortable. You can have the couch, I am sure it is as soft." She said swinging her legs up on to the large bed, stretching out.

"If you think I am going to sleep on this couch, without a mosquito net, in the middle of summer, you're crazy!"

"Well I am not sleeping with you!" Red said very strongly but made a conscious effort to keep her voice down with the open windows.

"Look nothing funny is going to happen, I am not that type of guy. Tell you what, if you like let's put these cushions from the two couches in the middle of the bed to separate it," James said holding up a large red rectangular plush cushion. "Will that be acceptable to you?"

"All right, all right, I don't like it but I don't really want you sick with a thousand mosquito bites either." Red said as they heard a soft knock at the door. Red opened it a crack to see a large man in a uniform with the hotel's name on his left jacket pocket.

"Hello, I was told you were robbed and could use a fresh change of clothes? I have a set of pants and a shirt for the gentleman and a dress for you. Both donated by staff of The Willard. Oh and I also have a night dress for you as well."

Red opened the door farther and smiled. "Thank you very much. Today has been a terrible experience."

"You don't know the half of it." James said inaudibly behind her. Red moved her leg back behind the door in a quick kick. James moved but not quite fast enough and her foot connected with his shin. "Owww." He said and took several steps back to rub his leg.

"Is there something wrong?" the porter asked.

"No, nothing is wrong. He bumped his leg on the table," she said taking the offered clothing in her hands, "thank you again."

"You are quite welcome Ma'am. If you need anything else go to the front desk. The lobby and front doors are closed but there will be someone on duty all night." He said inclining his head.

"That is very considerate, we will. Thank you again," she said closing the door.

"Now what was that for!" James said still rubbing his leg. While she didn't kick hard, and no damage was done, it still hurt.

"Watch what you say. You never know how well people can hear. Believe me, I have made that mistake before."

"You could have just said something, you didn't have to kick me."

"I wasn't sure of what you were going to say."

"You should know me better than that by now! I wasn't going to take any chances and say something that would cause us problems."

"All right, I am sorry. I won't do that again. Okay?"

"Apology accepted. Now let's get some sleep. Or try to in this heat. I for one want to get out of this time as soon as we can." James said pulling off his pants leaving only his loose fitting boxers.

"Here," Red said tossing him the pants and shirt. "I am going to change in the bathroom."

"Okay." James said as he caught the garments and sat them on the chair with the rest of his clothes. Walking over to the bed he sat the large cushions in the middle separating it. A moment later Red emerged from the bathroom wearing a long silk night gown. It looked more like a long white shirt that extended down past her knees with a little ruffle at the bottom. He smiled and quietly whistled.

"Oh be quiet," Red said rolling her eyes. "I could do the same for you, you know? White boxers and all."

James laughed. "Oh yeah right, I am nothing to drool over." He said pointing to his skinny muscle lacking frame. "Let me wash up in that bathroom."

"Be my guest," she said gesturing to the door.

A few moments later James emerged with a slight sound of water flushing in the background. "That is better. I was afraid they didn't have running water." He said pulling back the net and climbing on his side of the bed.

"Many places still don't. And I have a feeling this is one of the few hotels that do." Red slowly turned down the gas lamp until it finally went out, plunging the room into darkness. Almost immediately she heard the soft snores from James. But she lay thinking of how to pay for their bill in the morning. Nothing came to mind. She eventually rolled over to disappear into the world of dreams.

Sunlight streamed into the room and into Red's closed eyes. She covered her face with a pillow. "Ugh! Morning all ready?"

"Well well well, if it isn't sleeping beauty awake at last," James said smiling.

Red sat up and saw James already dressed in the white shirt and black pants given by the porter last night. "Why didn't you wake me?"

"You appeared to need it. And we are not in any hurry at the moment. And I think–"

But before he could finish the sentence a loud bang was heard in the distance. It was a deep sound that reverberated through the ground and into your bones. Then another, and a few moments later yet another.

"What in the world is *that*?" James jumped up wide-eyed.

"I have no idea. But if I didn't know better, I would say that is cannon fire."

"Cannon fire? In Washington D.C.? Can't be!"

"Well there were a few battles near the city during the Civil War, but I didn't think it was that close. Unless . . ."

"Unless what?"

"Have you been down to the front desk? Did you find out what the date is?"

James laughed. "You know me too well. Yes I did, it is July 11th 1864."

"July 11th? It must be the battle of Fort Stevens! It was the only battle during that time, and it was very close to the city."

"Then I think we had better get out of here as soon as possible."

"No, we still have our bill to deal with and I don't want to leave until that is settled."

"We could disappear. They could never follow us."

"Perhaps not, but it will leave a temporal loose end and I do not leave temporal loose ends. You never know what the effect might be. I will get dressed and we will go take a look at the battle."

"But isn't that dangerous? We just came out of one famous battle, and now you want to put us in another?"

Red laughed. "I am not going to 'put us in another' battle. I only want to see it. We are not going to get involved."

"Yeah right." James grunted as they left the room.

After managing to borrow the porter's horse, they went out in the direction of the gunfire. After a short ride they found the two sides clashed in battle. Cannon fire and guns were going off all around them as they left the horse to get a little closer on foot.

"Okay now we have seen it. Now can we go?" James said shaking his head.

"In a couple of minutes. Didn't you ever want to see the closest battle to Washington D. C. of the Civil War?"

"No! It is one reason I joined the FBI, to help prevent conflicts. Not go watch them."

"All right let's go ... wait a minute. Do you see what I see?"

James rolled his eyes. "Well I see a lot of men trying to kill each other. Do you see something else?"

"Yes that tall man over there," Red said pointing, "I think that is Abraham Lincoln."

"Abraham Lincoln? The President? Why would he be out in the middle of a battle? You must be mistaken." James stood squinting trying to make out what Red was pointing at.

"No look at that stance, his beard, that is him. Oh my–" Red's words were cut off as several men in confederate uniforms ran towards Lincoln's position. And he was clearly in the line of fire. "I have to stop them!" Red said as she started running.

"Red you can't ..." James started to say, but she was already some distance away and had shed the dress she was given only leaving her bodysuit. She covered the distance with incredible speed and shouted. "Mr. President! Get Down!" As she said it bullets began to zing through the air all around. Red dove headlong into Lincoln tackling and knocking him to the ground. A second later a man that was standing directly next to Lincoln went down holding his arm, blood gushing from a fresh bullet hole.

Several men ran forward their rifles pointed at Red. Lincoln looked up, his vision finally starting to resolve and realize what had happened. His face turned stormy when he saw the men's reaction. "Would you mind not pointing those firearms in my face and let me get up?"

"Yes sir, Mr. President." Several men said pulled Red to her feet then helped Lincoln to his. One of the officers pointed to Red and shouted "This woman ran into the President! She must be with the confederates! Take her away and have her executed!"

Lincoln's face grew even more enraged. "General! Just a moment! This woman saved my life. If it was not for her, I would be wearing the bullet hole that your surgeon now sports. Release her this minute!"

"But Sir, begging your pardon, she came out of nowhere. She could be with the confederates, a trick. I don't think–"

Lincoln cut him off. "General, am I not the President?"

The general saw where this was going and swallowed hard. "Yes."

"And as the President am I not your Commander-in-Chief?"

The General stiffened. "Yes Sir."

"Then as your Commander-in-Chief I order you to release this woman. Or I will have you relieved and incarcerated. Am I clear?"

The General nodded soberly. "Yes Sir," he turned to face his men, "release her, she is not with the confederates."

The men stiffed and nodded. "Yes Sir." Red shook herself upon release from the large two men that held her in a grip of iron.

Lincoln turned to Red. "I truly apologize for that," he said looking her up and down, "strange dress for a lady, but in any case I wish to know the name of the woman that saved my life, and wish to thank her personally."

Red raised her hand palm facing towards Lincoln. "My name is Red. And think nothing of it Mr. President. Your life was very much worth saving."

Lincoln smiled, took her hand anyway, and bowed somewhat. Not what she was expecting at all. "Still, I would like to thank you in some fashion," Lincoln's smile deepened.

"Well, first can we move farther back from the assault?

I know your snipers took out the people shooting in our direction, but it is still too close for comfort."

Lincoln laughed. "Of course, you are quite right. This way." He said gesturing to the road that led away from the conflict. After a few moments when they were well out of range he looked towards Red again. "Are you sure there is nothing I can do?"

"Well if you are insistent, there is a little matter of a bill at *The Willard*. We are passing through town and have a small bill there I was planning on settling today." By this time James had caught up to them and his face was flush with the excretion. "Oh and we borrowed the porter's horse. He is over there tied to a tree," Red said pointing to a far hill.

Lincoln stroked his beard. "*The Willard* you say? I know them well. Consider it taken care of."

"Are you sure?" Red asked. "I don't want to inconvenience you."

"My dear lady, you saved my life. And I am not the President after all? I think I can take care of a little hotel bill and have a horse returned." Lincoln said as he grabbed his horse, put a foot into a stirrup and swung his tall leg over.

"I am sure you can Sir."

"Please call me Abe, and if you need anything else, just let me know. You know where to find me." Lincoln said with a wink and road off for 1600 Pennsylvania Avenue.

Red and James continued off away from the city and conflict. After some time they found a wooded clearing. The grass covered area felt hard enough. "This will do," Red said. "Are you ready?"

"Yes. But I am surprised you tackled Lincoln like that. I mean it could have altered history. And I know how you are against any changes."

"Yes I am. But we know that Lincoln did not die then according to history. So there was no harm in making sure he didn't."

"But someone else should have, right? I mean we know he didn't die, so why did you intervene? Isn't it large risk with someone so prominent in history?"

"It is true the more important the person, the more interacting with them affects the time-line. But there is one thing you are not thinking of."

"Oh? And what would that be?"

"That perhaps I was supposed to do exactly what I did to prevent him from dieing today. If I didn't, history might have been changed."

"It what? You mean you have been here before?"

"Nope, never seen Lincoln before today."

"Then how–"

"I told you figuring out time travel can give you one massive headache. I do it all the time and I still don't have it figured out. It hurts too much." She said with a wink. "Now let's get going!" She bolted running in a clockwise direction faster and faster. The wind began to whip, and the trees swayed back and forth. She pushed increasing her speed again, lightning struck, and a crack in the very fabric of reality formed in the middle of the clearing. A large tree fell over at the edge of the wooded row. "Gooooo!" she shouted. James ran for the center and jumped into the warp with Red right behind him.

— 12 —

James felt the warp twist and pull. "Something is not right," he thought. He wanted to open his eyes, but dared not while inside a warp since the first time he inadvertently looked when traveling with Red caused him to empty the contents of his stomach right after.

James braced himself and opened his eyes. He saw the universe awash in color and light. Images flashed in front of his eyes. Possible futures, long past events, and he saw them all at once. His stomach churned, but he fought the terrible feeling and finally managed to gaze behind him.

Red was there, but her eyes were closed in deep concentration. He was about to look away when he saw her face flush and sweat started beading on her skin. She was having trouble. Then the whole warp shuddered and stretched. James almost lost control of every bodily function he had, but managed, somehow, to hold himself together. Red regained control, and the warp normalized. He wanted to tell her to create an exit point, anywhere, it didn't matter. She couldn't keep this up. But he also knew that if he disturbed her concentration, even for a second, while inside the warp, they might not make it out again ...ever. And it was taking all she had just keeping the warp stable.

James forced himself to look away. He saw a faint change in the color scape off in the distance. Not much but perhaps enough. He closed his eyes and concentrated on that point. "We must go there ...we must exit." He repeated over and over again. Using every ounce of will he had, he concentrated on that point. He couldn't see the point shudder and grow in size and their direction shift towards it. He continued to concentrate hoping his mind could have an effect on the warp at least in some small way.

The point neared them and burst open ripping open a gash in the fabric of space-time. It then grew in size and began to draw them closer sucking them into itself. James felt something about to consume them and hoped it was a good situation but dared not look.

James felt himself hurled out of the warp and hit a brick wall. "OOF." He shouted and turned around in time to see Red follow him out and catch her before she crashed into the wall herself. The warp behind them, an angry mass of convoluted energy folded in on itself, disappearing as though it had never been.

Red lay in his arms unconscious. Looking around, they were in another alleyway between two large brick buildings about the same general construction as their last jump. "Must be about the same time period," James muttered. Looking down Red was still not moving. He held her up and shook softly. "Red? Red? Are you all right?" No response. He put his head down by her heart and heard its soft steady beat. Her breaths came in calm and steady as well. Whatever happened, she was alive and seemed okay otherwise, but he was no doctor.

James held her close and started walking toward the alley entrance. The air was warm but had a touch of autumn in it and the smell of coal and tobacco smoke hung in the air. It and the filth of the alleyway felt like Washington all over again. But the buildings looked slightly different. James couldn't put his finger on the type, but he knew they had changed. He walked out onto the cobble stone street and saw several horse drawn carriages that he recognized instantly. "England! We must be in England!" he whispered to himself.

A horse whinnied and James turned to find a cab barreling down upon them. He tried to move back but thankfully the horse saw him beforehand and bucked up shoving the cab back a bit. The driver on the top shouted "Whoooah easy boy easy." Then looked at James. "Hey! Watch where you are going! You could have–"

"Driver what is going on?" A voice called from inside the cab.

"Sorry sir, this man came out of nowhere and stood in front of us."

"So I see." The man inside said leaning forward and opening the large side door exposing the leather interior of the cab. "I say are you all right? What is wrong with the lady? We didn't hit her did we?"

James looked at Red then the gentleman inside the cab. "Oh not at all. I am not sure what is wrong with her. And forgive me for disturbing you, I didn't see you."

"You don't know what is wrong with her?"

"No. She looked fatigued and then collapsed. Her heart and breathing are strong, so I am not sure what the problem is."

"I see. Well bring her into my cab and we will take her to my office, it is only a few blocks from here."

"She needs a doctor, I don't–"

The man smiled. His wide handlebar mustache framing his

even wider grin. "Sir, I am a doctor. Please let me take a look at her. It is the least I can do."

James smiled then nodded. "Thank you." He said while carefully setting Red in the seat then climbed in next to her.

The man smiled and offered his hand. "My name is Doyle."

James took his hand. "Call me James and thank you again."

Doyle smiled again. "Think nothing of it. We will have your lady fixed up in no time." He tapped the ceiling of the cab with his cane. "DRIVER! My office please."

"Yes sir." The driver responded, and they were off listening to the soft clip-clop of shod hooves on cobblestone streets.

A few minutes later the cab stopped in front of a building with a sign by the door that read *Doctor George Budd Practicing Physician*. James looked at the sign and pointed. "Umm, I thought you said your name was Doyle?"

Doyle laughed and opened the cab getting out. "I am. That is my partners name. My office is inside down the hall from his." He paused and raised his hands in offering. "Let me help you get her inside."

"No, that is quite all right. I can manage. Thank you for offering." James said while taking Red into his arms, carefully got out of the cab. Doyle flipped a coin up to the driver. Both men nodded to each other, the driver twitched his horse, and they trotted off.

Inside, the building was quite lavishly decorated with comfortable chairs in the waiting room. Each one was filled to capacity but Doyle passed them all without so much as a glance and led James to the back room. He pulled out his key, unlocked the door and gestured for James to enter.

"Set her on my examination couch over there." Doyle pointed to a well padded sofa that been elevated to better suit examination.

"But all your other patients?" James inquired as he carefully laid her on the examination couch.

Doyle laughed again. "They are not mine. They are my partners. You two are my first this week. I haven't been practicing that long. And before you ask, yes I graduated." He said pointing to a certificate on the wall. "With high honors I might add. Now let's have a look at your lady. What is her name by the way?"

"Red." James said as a look of great concern washed over his face.

"Red? Unusual name for such a pretty lady." Doyle said as he took her wrist and felt her pulse. "You are right her pulse is strong. Get my bag over there." He said pointing to a large black leather satchel resting on a set of cabinets. James nodded and handed him the bag. Doyle pulled out various tools including a stethoscope, which he promptly placed in either ear and listened to Red's heart and lungs. "Her heart sounds good as do her lungs." He looked into her eyes then covered one for a few minutes then uncovered it looking again with a magnifying lens. "Pupils are acting normally." Using a small rubber hammer he tapped Red in several locations. "Reflexes are responding. What were you doing before she collapsed?"

"Well …" James said thinking quickly. "We were walking along and she looked flushed as though under a great strain. I managed to help her out but then she became unresponsive as you now see."

Doyle's eyebrow raised. "I see. Well I am not finding anything unusual. I can try some smelling salts to see if that brings her around?"

James gazed down at Red, placed his hand on her forehead rubbing with his thumb slightly, then looked up with his face full of concern not knowing what to do. He finally nodded. "All right."

Doyle went to a cabinet and removed a small glass bottle. He walked back over to Red's sleeping form, uncorked the bottle, and waved it under her nose. Immediately she sat up coughed gagged and shouted "What the heck is that! It smells terrible!"

James chuckled. "I guess she will make it."

Red frowned at James. "What do you mean guess I will make it? I am fine I ..." Then the room started to spin, and she lay back down.

"With all due respect, you are not fine. While I don't see a reason for your unconsciousness, we couldn't wake you with the normal methods. I was forced to use smelling salts. Since that did work, I suspect now all you need is a good meal and a rest. Then you will be fine," Doyle said smiling.

When the room finally slowed down, she focused on the strange man standing next to her. "And who are you?"

"My name is Arthur Doyle and I am a doctor. James here was concerned about you. Since my cab almost ran you over, I offered to examine you at my office."

"Doctor? Run us down? I don't ... understand." She said as the room started to spin again.

"It is a long story. I will tell you later." James gripped her hand. "Don't worry I am here. You will be okay. Just need some rest I think."

Doyle smiled. "It is almost time for tea. I will go get us some. If you would like to join me that is?"

"Oh we wouldn't want to intrude." James said not taking his eyes off of Red.

"No intrusion at all. And in fact I insist. I will be back shortly." Doyle said as he slipped out a side door.

James leaned close. "You gave me quite a scare. I am glad you are okay."

Red looked at him, or tried to. "I will be once the room stops spinning. This guy almost ran us down?"

"Yes I was carrying you. We landed in some back alley. When I got to the main street, his cab was about to our location. We were not in any real danger, they don't go that fast. The cab stopped in plenty of time. One advantage of having an intelligent animal powering a vehicle."

Red gripped the side of the couch as the room finally started to slow its relentless spin. "Doesn't sound like we traveled very far in time then. Horse drawn cabs?"

"Not in time, but I think we traveled distance. This appears to be England. Not sure what time. But judging by the good doctors equipment late, 1800s."

Red sat up against James' protests. "I am okay. The room is almost back to normal now. A little rest and I will be fine. But I am not up to nosing around. Look around this office. I want to know who was examining me."

"He didn't do much other than check your heart and respiration."

"Well I still want to know!" Red said in hushed tones. "It is always good to know who you are interacting with on a jump. Or have you forgotten that?"

"No I haven't forgotten," James said as he looked around the room, "interesting."

"What?" Red said trying to sit up, but the room spun again and she lay back down.

"He has a copy of *A Study In Scarlet* on his desk."

"*A Study In Scarlet?* Why does that sound familiar?"

"It is a story with Sherlock Holmes. What is really odd though is this copy is hand written."

Red said up with a start "What? You idiot, this doctor must be Conan Doyle."

"Can't be. He said his name was Arthur."

"Yes Sir Arthur Conan Doyle. Well will be eventually."

"Oh wow you are right." James said slapping his forehead. "I forgot his full name."

"Yes. He dropped the Arthur part of his name at some point but we never knew when. *A Study In Scarlet* was his first work with Sherlock Holmes. This is one critical point in history. Do you realize how much influence this man's work has had over the years? We need to get out of here."

"I am sure it is. But as long as we don't convince him not to publish, what can be the harm?"

Red sighed and shook her head then wished she didn't. "I don't know. Sometimes the course of events seems so predictable. Then the slightest deviation destroys the whole time-line."

"Or reaffirms it. You said yourself that there are moments when you suspect you have done something before or fixed history to happen the way it was supposed to."

"Sometimes, not very often though. But you need to understand those points I didn't have a choice and ended up in the middle of a bad situation. This one we do have a choice and need to leave ... *now*."

"I don't think that would be a good idea. He would get suspicious, remember this is the guy that created Sherlock Holmes. Why not stay and have tea then leave quietly?"

Red snorted. "You have a point there. Okay, but try not to do anything. Even the smallest change could have a huge impact at such a critical point."

The side door popped open and Doyle appeared with a silver tray containing tea, sandwiches, and several kinds of small cakes or baked goods. "I thought you were only bringing tea?" James said as he leapt forward to help Doyle with the door.

"This is normal tea. Don't tell me you never had a normal English tea this time of day?" Doyle said his right eyebrow raising.

James smiled. "Yes, of course, but I thought you were bringing only tea considering we are strangers. And I didn't want to impose."

Doyle sat the tray down upon a waist-high bookshelf. "Well even strangers deserve a proper tea. And I told you, you are not imposing at all."

"It does look good I admit." Red said gazing at the tray and starting to swing her legs over the side of the couch.

Doyle pointed. "You lie back and rest, doctor's orders. I will bring it to you." He poured tea in a fine china cup with a well-practiced hand, placed it on a saucer with a small sandwich and passed it to Red. "There you are."

Red nodded slightly taking them. "Thank you."

"You are welcome." Doyle said as he passed a cup to James, then made one for himself.

"I don't know how we can repay you." James said while munching on a sandwich.

Doyle raised his hand and shook his head as he sat down in a well padded chair. "I told you don't worry about it. It is I who should apologize as my cab almost ran you over. Besides as I mentioned, you are my first patient all week."

"I don't understand that. If your partner has all the patients …"

"Well, let's say his methods are not mine. And I prefer to use my own. They may not get me as many patients quickly, but I know they will come in time. And my practice will be better for it in the long run," Doyle said sipping his tea.

James noticed that Red had already eaten her sandwich, and he passed her another. "I wish to thank you again for your kindness. I am feeling better all the while."

"I'm very relieved to hear that. I figured you only need a little time." Doyle said finishing his tea. "I would like to prescribe you some pills though. They will help should you have another one of these weak periods." He said walking over to his desk. Shuffling through several stacks of papers he took the copy of *A Study In Scarlet* and threw it in the trash bin alongside his desk.

Red and James' eyes grew wide in astonishment. "If I may, what was that big stack of papers you threw out?" Red asked while pointing to the bin.

"Oh that? It is a story I wrote to pass the time waiting between patients. Nothing of any concern." He said flipping through several other stacks producing a small envelope with thirty or so white pills. "Ah here they are. I had another patient that didn't want them after I had already filled out the prescription. Take one if you are feeling faint and it should help." He said handing the small white envelope to Red.

"Thank you," Red said, "but if I may, why did you throw the story out? Is it not any good?"

"Well every publisher I have tried seems to not want it. Why should I?" Doyle shrugged.

"Mind if I read it?" James asked.

"Not at all. Keep it if you like."

James grabbed the stack of paper from the bin and read through the first few pages. "This is very good. I think you should keep trying. I am sure someone will want to publish it. I know I would buy it if I saw it." James handed the stack back to Doyle.

"You really think so? I thought it had to be lacking, if publishers didn't want it."

"I suspect it is not a matter of them not liking it, but not wanting to take a chance on an unpublished author. You need to keep trying. Once you get started, the next will be much easier," Red said smiling.

Doyle walked back over to his desk and placed *A Study In Scarlet* back on the ink blotter where it was before. "I think you are probably right. The same with my practice. It all takes time."

"Yes it does," James said nodding.

Red sat up and James rushed over to help her to her feet. "I am feeling much better doctor and I wish to thank you again for your help. We must be going."

Doyle nodded. "If those pills don't help or you have any other symptoms, please do call again."

"We will. Thank you." James said as they left Doyle's office and worked their way past all the other patients to the front street. "Whew another case of we helped history along?" James said once they were alone.

Red rolled her eyes. "More like a case of we saved the time-line from our contamination. I doubt he would have thrown the story in the trash had we not been here. It looked like a last minute impulse."

"Perhaps," James said keeping a firm grip on Red should she start to feel ill again. "Or perhaps not. I think we were supposed to be here."

"Believe what you like. And what in the world happened with that last jump? The last thing I remembered was jumping ahead and the next ending up in Doyle's office."

"I am not sure. The warp was acting strangely and twisting in on itself. I could see many different histories and probable futures at once. When I looked back you were flushed and looked fatigued. Then the warp fluctuated again, and you looked worse."

"Hmm then we crashed out?" Red nodded.

"Not exactly."

"What do you mean 'not exactly'?"

"Well … the warp seemed to be destabilizing yet we weren't exiting. Felt almost like we were stuck, or the warp was breaking down around us. I looked ahead and saw a small point that might have been a hole or something. I closed my eyes and focused on being there. Next thing I knew, I hit a brick wall … literally. Then turned around and caught you. You were unconscious at the time."

"You? You guided our exit? Not possible!"

"I don't know. All I know is what I told you. I had a feeling that if I didn't try, we wouldn't have made it."

"And you mentioned you saw things inside the warp?"

"Yes all colors and images of history present and future at once. It was very confusing. I couldn't tell if it was something I actually saw or something in my minds eye."

Red shook her head. "Actually both are the same when in the warp. What you see in your mind tends to guide the outcome. It takes a great deal of concentration and practice to wrangle some sort of control of it. I can't imagine that you managed it. But yet here we are. And I know I did not guide us this time. At least not to an exit point. We should have crashed out though if there was a problem. At least that is what has always happened in the past."

"I know. It is odd. Now what do we do?"

"We find a place to stay for the next few nights and rest. I obviously haven't been resting enough, and I must before we try again."

James nodded. "But where? And if you haven't noticed, there are a lot of people staring in your direction."

"I don't know. We only need a couple of days. Shouldn't be too hard. And yes I noticed, I am dressed rather unusual for this period. Something else we need to fix." Reds eyes lit up upon seeing a *BOARDERS WANTED* sign in a window and pointed. "Now that looks promising."

James rolled his eyes. "May I remind you we don't have 1800s money, much less English pounds."

"We may not need it. Follow me." Red knocked first then entered the old Victorian home with James right behind her. The entry way was decently furnished and an older lady came out wearing a long dress. She wiped her hands on her apron and greeted them.

"Hello. I am Mrs. Hudson. How can I help you?" She said gazing at Red, her eyes going up and down.

"My name is Red, and this is James. We saw your sign and are interested in a place to stay for a couple of nights."

"I see. Well I was looking for long-term boarders as I am not a hotel. But I have a set of three furnished rooms upstairs you can use for a guinea a day," Mrs. Hudson said still shifting her gaze.

"That would be fine except . . . "

"Yes?"

"We had a problem and don't have a shilling between us at the moment," Red said looking down at the floor.

Mrs. Hudson's nose wrinkled even more than usual and she seemed lost in thought for a moment. "I see. And would this explain your very scandalous attire?" Red nodded then Mrs. Hudson's eyes widened. "Were you robbed?"

Red hesitated. "Yes I am afraid so. If it wasn't for James, I am not sure what would have happened."

"You poor dears. If you can help me around here, you can stay for a couple of days. Mr. Hudson died last year, and it has been difficult for me to keep the place up all by myself. I am falling behind and haven't had the money to pay for such things as cleaning the chimneys or the stove pipes."

James stepped forward. "I am sorry for your loss and I would be happy to help you Mrs. Hudson."

Mrs. Hudson smiled. "Thank you dear. I assume the robbers didn't leave you with any of your belongings?"

Red shook her head. "No. They took everything."

"Well I can't have people working around here looking like that. I have an old dress that I think might fit you. And Mr. James is welcome to anything that Mr. Hudson left. I have no use for it currently."

James bowed slightly. "We thank you for your generosity Mrs. Hudson."

"There is an old trunk upstairs second door on the left which should have something for you. And I will get a dress for you Miss Red. Or is that Mrs.?"

"Just Red is fine thank you," Red said smiling.

Mrs. Hudson's eyebrows raised. "All right dear, follow me." Mrs. Hudson showed Red down the hall to her room on the first floor. It was elegantly furnished with thick carpeting. Whoever Mr. Hudson was, he obviously had a good income at one time. She opened a wardrobe and found an older dress in the back and held it up to Red. "I think this will do. You are a mite taller than I am, but it should fit in all the important areas," she said smiling.

"Yes this will be fine. Thank you." Red took the dress and began unfastening the back. It was long and black with a lace area at the top framing the collarbone area ending in a high neckline.

As Red stepped into the dress, Mrs. Hudson got behind her. "Let me help you dear, I know how difficult they are to fasten by yourself." After a few minutes, Red was fully enclosed in several layers of fabric leading her to wonder how women of this time period ever got any work done at all. The dress was a little short, resting a few inches below her knees, but fit well everywhere else.

A few moments later they met James in the hallway. He was in a simple white shirt and long pants with a matching jacket. "I thank you for the loan Mrs. Hudson. They fit remarkably well."

Mrs. Hudson seemed to not hear James for a few minutes then shook her head as if to break a spell. "Sorry Mr. James, I was remembering the last time Mr. Hudson wore that. I am glad it fits. If you will help me with the two fireplaces upstairs that would be wonderful. They haven't been swept for a long time."

"Of course," James said nodding, "show me where."

Mrs. Hudson looked to Red. "Wait for me in the kitchen dear, it is the second door over there." Red nodded and left as Mrs. Hudson led James upstairs to a set of rooms. It was obvious that this was rented by someone else judging by all the papers on the table in the center. James could smell tobacco smoke rather strongly and the slight hint of creosote. Looking at the fireplace itself though, it seemed rather clean.

"I don't understand. It seems clean."

"Not down here, the flue. It hasn't been swept since Mr. Hudson passed and the draft is failing." She said handing him a large chimney brush and folded cloth. "Make sure you use the cloth to catch the soot. If you have any problems, let me know." She turned and left with her bustled dress wiggling slightly in her wake.

James looked up the flu and realized he would have to get inside the fireplace and try to clean it from there. But that would really make a mess of himself and the room no matter if used the cloth or not. He thought about other possible methods, but nothing would work in this time. His eyes widened with an idea. He removed the gun from its hidden holster and opened the grip control pad. Keying in the ultrasonic setting, he then activated the stealth mode. The gun beeped slightly with confirmation and closed the control panel. He smiled and fired.

Red was busy cleaning the kitchen stove when she thought she heard something odd and turned to Mrs. Hudson who was in the middle of preparing dinner for her other tenants. "Did you just hear something?"

"No I didn't. What did you hear?"

"It sounded like a faint whine."

"I didn't hear anything, but then these ears are not what they used to be." She pointed to an ear with a flour coated finger.

"I am going to check on James. I will be right back." Red said putting down her cleaning brush.

Mrs. Hudson nodded. "Okay dear, but be quick. I need that stove clean soon. My other tenants will arrive in a few hours."

Red went up stairs and found James walking out of a room with a grin as large as a Cheshire Cat. "Okay what did you do?"

"Me? I didn't do anything?"

"That grin tells me otherwise. And I heard something odd

downstairs. Sounded like a soft whine. I almost didn't catch it."

James continued his smile. "Oh I was cleaning."

"Cleaning? Nothing whines like that in this century. What did you do?" Her eyes widened suddenly. "You didn't use the gun did you?"

"I did, but only on stealth mode. The ultrasonic disruptor setting really worked well. I bet Mrs. Hudson has never had such a clean chimney."

"Stealth mode? Since when does it have a stealth mode?"

"It is only available for some settings. The more powerful modes can't use it." James said padding his jacket with the gun safely hidden underneath.

"It could use some work. I heard it. You took one heck of a risk no one would see it."

James rolled his eyes. "You yourself said it was only a slight whine, no one but you would have realized what it was or bother investigating it. And I did lock the door before I used it. No one saw or heard a thing."

Red snorted. "So you say."

"Look would you rather try to help clean me up from being covered head to toe in soot without the aid of a shower?"

Red frowned. "Okay, you have a point there. Just be careful with that thing."

"I know, I know, I won't damage the time-line. Trust me," James smiled.

"See that you don't." Red smiled and gave him a quick squeeze before heading back down to the kitchen.

Later that night Red and James ate with Mrs. Hudson. Her usual tenants didn't arrive for dinner and it was only the three of them. Eating in silence, it was Mrs. Hudson who spoke first. "That was a wonderful job you did on the chimneys. I don't think I have ever had them so clean. And so quickly too. I also expected to find a large mess of the rooms as the last chimney sweep made, but it looked just as I left it. You must tell me your secret."

James thought quickly. "I used to help sweep for a friends business and he shared uh, a few special methods. And I promised I would never reveal them."

"I see. Well far be it from me to make you break a promise. I will make sure to call you next time," Mrs. Hudson said with a smile.

After dinner Red and James left for their room. Also well furnished as was the rest of the house, but there was only one bed. James sighed. "I will sleep on the couch in the other room. It should be comfortable enough."

"It is okay, don't worry about it. Grab a few cushions and set them in the middle like before."

James shook his head. "Slight problem there. They are attached to the couch. Don't worry about it I will be fine."

"You need the sleep as much as I do. She had you running all over today. I think she worked you far harder than I."

"Well she hasn't had a man around helping her for over a year. I don't think the women of this time period do much at all." He sat down rubbing and stretching trying to get a kink out of his shoulder.

"No they generally don't do much heavy manual labor. Women were seen as the weaker sex at this point. And like I said, you take half of the bed okay?"

"All right. I am not going to argue with you tonight. I am too tired."

"See? I was right."

"Maybe."

Red snorted. "Maybe? What do you mean maybe?"

James held up his hands. "Nothing at all." He said taking off the uncomfortable shoes and belt. Then removing all but his undershirt and shorts.

"James?" Red said smiling

"Yes?"

"Can you do me a favor?"

"Of course. What is it?"

"Get me out of this thing!" She said gesturing to the tight restrictive dress she had been in all day.

James laughed quietly. "Of course." He spun her around undoing fasteners and loosening several laces.

Red let out a huge sigh letting the tight dress, a mass of fabric and lace fall to the floor. "Thank you. It is no wonder women of this time period didn't do a lot. These clothes wouldn't let them."

"Are you going to sleep in your bodysuit tonight?" James said pointing.

"No. Thankfully Mrs. Hudson gave me a long night dress. I am going to change in the wash room. And no peeking." She said with a grin.

James snorted. "M'lady I would never peek."

"I know." Red said playfully as she closed the door. When she emerged she looked refreshed, dressed in a long night dress that just reached her knees. "I am glad Mrs. Hudson and I are only different in height and what are you doing?" She said pointing to James who was holding her dress and half inside a large wardrobe.

"What do you think? Hanging up your dress. I have a feeling that Mrs. Hudson would kick up a fuss if she found it all wrinkled in the morning."

"You are probably right. Let's get some sleep. I have a feeling tomorrow is going to be another long day."

"Agreed." James said pulling the covers down on the bed and climbing in.

Red nodded turned down the lamp until it was finally out. Moonlight streamed in from the side window as she climbed into the bed. She could already hear James soft snores. Thoughts of the past few days played through her mind over and over as she tried to make sense of them. Finally she sighed and turned over falling asleep.

Red awoke to a knocking at the door. "Red? Can you help me with breakfast please?" Mrs. Hudson called. It took her a few moments to realize where she was. She looked over and James was starting to open his eyes.

"Yes of course Mrs. Hudson. I will get changed and meet you in the kitchen shortly," Red answered.

"Thank you dear," Mrs. Hudson said.

"Well James I think it is time we get to work."

"Mmmm? Work … too early," he grumbled, "it is not even light outside." He said throwing the blanket over his head.

"Come on sleepy head," Red cooed and padded his blanketed hip, "you remember what we promised Mrs. Hudson?"

"Yes. But not this early," he grumbled back.

"All right, tell you what you help me into my dress then I will let you sleep a bit more. Deal?"

James' head popped up from under the covers. "Okay deal."

Red quickly rushed into the rest room to wash and change into some Victorian underwear that Mrs. Hudson has graciously provided yesterday. When she emerged, she found James holding her dress out ready for her to step into. "Okay let's get this over with." She sighed stepping into the multilayered garment. After a several minutes James had her fastened, and the laces drawn.

"There you go. Now I am going to sleep a little more. I will meet you downstairs later."

"If I cook breakfast for you, you had better be there." Red said placing her hands on her hips and tapping her foot.

James laughed. "Of course I will. Although I don't think I have ever had your cooking until now. Might be dangerous." He said with a wink before flopping back into bed.

"Very funny Mr. Sleepyhead, you just wait."

"Mmmmmm hmmmmmm." James hummed before he dozed off again.

A little over an hour later James stumbled into the kitchen, dressed but still looking a little groggy. "Well well well, look who finally got up," Red said smiling.

"Hello Mr. James. Did you have a rough night?" Mrs. Hudson asked.

"Not at all. Actually a good one. I admit having trouble waking up this morning. Give me a little time." He sniffed the air. "Do I smell coffee?"

"Yes," Mrs. Hudson said while continuing to knead some dough, "while I don't usually make it, Red said you might appreciate it this morning."

"Indeed I would," James said smiling. He looked around for the pot but Red had already poured him a cup and placed it on the small table.

"There you are. Drink it and Mrs. Hudson has a few short jobs for you to do. Breakfast won't be for another hour."

"Thank you," James looked up and blinked, "another hour?"

"Yes, I am making rolls and other items I normally don't bother with. But since I have help today ..." Mrs. Hudson said smiling and started to separate the kneaded dough into long slender snakes. "Red give him the list I pinned to the pantry door over there." She said nodding in the direction of a small hand written note affixed to the door with a sewing needle.

Red handed James the list, and he looked it over and frowned when he got halfway down the list. "Replace shingles?"

Mrs. Hudson sighed. "Yes I saw a few shingles have fallen off in the past month or so and they need to be fixed before winter. Mr. Hudson did keep spares in the basement along with his ladder. And you might as well fix the lamp when you are down there. It failed a few months ago as well."

It was James' turn to sigh then rubbed his forehead. "Okay, I will do my best. But how will I see down there if the normal lamp is broken?"

"I have another lantern you can use. There is one in the hall closet, on the right as you enter." Mrs. Hudson said as she placed several snakes of dough onto a large metal sheet then turned to Red. "Is the oven ready?"

"Yes, Mrs. Hudson."

"Good, open it I want to slide these in."

James drank the last of his coffee and stood up. "I'll get to work on this list and start with the lantern in the basement. Red, come get me when breakfast is ready."

"Of course," she said nodding then closing the oven and adding another piece of wood to the firebox on the side.

A little less than an hour later Red went to the basement stairs and found James at the entrance with a lantern in several sections. "Breakfast is ready. Having trouble?"

James scratched his head. "Yes I have taken this thing all

apart, cleaned it and put it back together three times and it still does not work. Doesn't make sense."

"Did you try trimming the wick?"

James looked up with a start. "You are kidding right? It couldn't be that simple?" He pulled out a knife, removed a good half inch from the wick and reassembled the lantern. "Hand me that box of matches over there will you?" he said pointing.

"Sure." Red flipped him the box which he caught in midair, stuck a match and applied it to the wick. Immediately the fire took, and the lamp glowed brightly.

"Well I'll be. It didn't look sooty," he looked to Red. "How did you know?"

Red smiled. "You forget I have been jumping for a bit longer than you have. Now we had better get to the dinning room before the food gets cold and Mrs. Hudson gets mad at us."

"Agreed.   And what you two were cooking smells wonderful," James said as his stomach rumbled.

The dinning room table was laid out with sausages, eggs, tea, biscuits, small loves of bread and fresh butter. James sat down and ate hungrily, but not rudely. "This is wonderful. Thank you Mrs. Hudson."

"I am glad you are enjoying it. And I didn't do it alone, I had a lot of help." She smiled looking toward Red.

"Yes, I churned that butter you are inhaling," Red said her eyes narrowing.

James smiled "It is very good, and I am not eating that fast."

Red smiled back "I know."

"She did a lot more than churn the butter. Keeping the oven at the proper temperature for long periods is tricky. And she did a wonderful job."

Red inclined her head sightly towards Mrs. Hudson. "Thank you."

"You are welcome dear. James, how is the list coming?"

"Well I will try to have it all done. But I am off to a slow start, fixing the lantern took longer than I thought."

"Oh don't worry about it dear." Mrs. Hudson said with a wave of her hand. "Mr. Hudson always had trouble with that one too. He did eventually get it going though. And why it has sat unused for so long."

James looked around at the empty chairs and realized that the other tenants hadn't arrived. "Mrs. Hudson, where are the other boarders? I thought you said you were expecting them?"

"I was. I received a telegram 10 minutes ago that they wouldn't be back until late tomorrow. I wish he would give me more warning of his plans. Don't worry about the extra, we will save it for lunch if you agree?"

James sat back and made a sigh of satisfaction. "Of course. It was wonderful. No complaints here." He said standing up as his tea was finished. "Well I had best get back to the list if I am going to get it all done by tonight. Thank you again."

"You are welcome dear." Mrs. Hudson said as she and Red began to clear the table.

Later that night James slowly entered their room with slouched shoulders and found Red already there sitting on one of the couches. "Are you okay?"

"I think so. I sure hope you are resting up because I am working harder than I have in my whole life."

"Yes I am. We will be ready to go tomorrow I am sure."

"Good." He said moving over to the bed leaving a line of clothes in his wake. "I am tired of fixing roofs, lanterns, chopping firewood, cleaning more chimneys, and putting up storm windows. Mrs. Hudson missed her calling, she should have been an FBI trainer."

Red's eyes widened. "You did all that today?"

"Yes and more. Mrs. Hudson thought of a few other things this afternoon," he said practically falling into bed.

"James?"

"Yes?"

"Aren't you forgetting something?"

He sat up thinking for a moment. "Oh God I hope not. I don't want to go back out there."

"No. ME!" She said gesturing to her dress.

"Ohhhh," James chuckled as he stood up and walked over to Red, "sorry I totally forgot." He said as he began to unfasten her dress and loosen its long laces.

"Shhh don't worry about it. I know how tired you are." She felt the final fastener release, and she took a deep breath. "Ohh thank you."

"You're welcome. Need any more help with it?"

"No, that's enough. I will get changed in the bathroom."

"Okay, and I will crash out here." He said sitting down on the bed wondering if he had the strength to lay down.

A moment later Red emerged in her night dress. "Oh does that feel better. You guys really had it made in the clothing department in this time."

James had managed to lay down. "Yes," he said groggily, "I guess so."

"What do you mean you guess so?" She said turning to look at him but he didn't respond, already fast asleep. Red smiled as she pulled the cover over him, tucked him in, gave a slight squeeze and whispered "good-night," in his ear before putting out the lamp.

Morning came far too early with Mrs. Hudson's usual wake up call. James groaned and rolled over pulling the pillow over his head. Red was already awake and beginning to put the dress back on. "James would you please help me? I can't get this thing on without you."

"Of course. One sec." He grumbled and sat up trying to get his eyes to focus. After a few minutes he managed to move his complaining body over to Red, cinched her dress closed and fastened it. "There. That okay?"

"As okay as this thing gets. Thank you. You rest a bit. I know you haven't recovered from yesterday. I will take care of the morning chores okay?"

"Okay," he said flopping back upon the bed, "but if it is anything heavy, hard or such you come and get me. Deal?" He mumbled into a pillow.

"Of course," she said smiling but his soft snores could already be heard. Red headed down to the kitchen where Mrs. Hudson was waiting.

"Hello dear," then she noticed James was not with her, "I see Mr. James is not with you. Is he all right?"

"Yes he is fine, but didn't sleep very well last night. I told him he could rest until breakfast. I hope that is okay?"

"Oh the poor dear. And that is fine. He did a lot yesterday, I wasn't planning on giving him another list for today. Unless you plan on staying another day?"

"Sadly we need to be going. But we thank you for your wonderful hospitality."

"It is I who should be thanking you. I don't know how I would have got ready for winter without James' help. Shall we make another batch of the rolls and biscuits he liked so well? You can take it with you when you go."

Red nodded her eyes glowing. "Yes I am sure he would like that. Shall I get the oven up to temperature?"

"Yes dear, you do that. And I will start the biscuits."

Sometime later James awoke to the most wonderful smells filling the air. Biscuits, eggs, fresh butter, and rolls wafted to his nose. He sat up shook the last bit of sleep from his head and proceeded to get dressed. A few minutes later Red entered the bedroom smiling.

"I see you are up. Did you get my gentle wake up call?"

"If you mean the wonderful smells, who could sleep through that?"

Red's smile broadened. "I thought it would be more gentle than me trying to wake the dead."

"Very funny," James said, "I see it's your turn to be the comedian."

Red's eyes flashed. "Perhaps. Come down to the dining room when you are ready."

A few moments later James entered the dining room. The table was again filled with wonderful food, the smell of which made his stomach rumble. But like yesterday, he didn't see any other tenants. Mrs. Hudson sat at the head of the elegant table as usual with Red right next to her, but no one else. "The other tenants won't be joining us?"

Mrs. Hudson shook her head. "They won't return until later this afternoon."

"Then you made too much for our breakfast." James said as he waved over the small banquet that was in front of them.

"Don't worry dear, I didn't do it alone. And I thought you might like to take it with you. Red says you have a long journey ahead of you."

James nodded. "That we do."

After breakfast Red helped with the dishes and James went

up to the room to put their freshly washed clothes into the large shoulder bag Mrs. Hudson had given them. He thought about how hard this time was, but there was something different about the people here. He gazed out on to the street below, his stare distant. He would miss Mrs. Hudson and hoped she would be all right. When he finally got downstairs, he found them both by the door waiting.

"All ready dear?" Mrs. Hudson said pointing to the bag slung over his shoulder.

"Yes," he said padding the bag "I have everything. Not that it is much."

"Well not everything." Red said giving him a large grin and passed several items from breakfast meticulously wrapped in a layered cloth.

"Ohhhhh yes. And thank you again Mrs. Hudson." He said nodding while placing them carefully in the bag.

"You are welcome dear. Now there is something else I want you to have." She said holding out her hand, James reached out, and she placed several coins in his hand. "It is not much, but it is enough to start your travels with."

James shook his head handing the money back. "Mrs. Hudson we can't accept this."

Mrs. Hudson closed his hand around the coins and held it tightly in hers. "Please take it. I don't know how I would have been ready for winter without your help. It would have cost me far more than this."

James started to shake his head when Red placed her hand on the middle of his back and tapped, then giving him a look. "Thank you again Mrs. Hudson. We are truly honored."

"Yes Mrs. Hudson," James nodded, "we are honored."

"You are welcome dears. Now you had best be on your way."

They both nodded in agreement and walked out the front door. Gazing back they saw Mrs. Hudson waving slightly with a large smile on her wrinkled face then she closed the sizable door. James waved for a cab and instructed the driver to take them to the edge of the city. The driver gave an odd look but when James tossed one of the coins to him he nodded.

It was some time before James turned to Red. "I don't understand why we had to accept the money."

"You forget, in this time it would have been a large insult if we didn't. Almost as though she wasn't worthy to give us anything."

"Oh my, I certainly didn't mean it that way!"

"I know you didn't. And notice I didn't kick you this time," Red said smiling.

"Yes I noticed. Thank you."

"Now can you do me a favor?"

"Yes?"

"Get me out of this thing!"

James chuckled starting to unfasten her dress. "Of course."

"Quit laughing Mr. I-can-wear-pants." Red said as she grabbed the shoulder bag and took out her bodysuit. "And no peeking."

James eyes widened. "I wouldn't do that! You should know–"

Red smiled and placed a finger on his lips. "I know."

After some time the cab arrived at the edge of town. The roads had changed to more dirt than cobblestone and nothing could be seen but trees and grass in any direction. "Sir, we are at the edge of town. I don't see anything here. Do you wish me to continue on or go somewhere else?" the driver called.

"No, this is fine. Thank you." James said emerging from the cab and helped Red out.

"But there is no one here." The driver said gesturing to the wide area that was devoid of anyone.

"We are waiting for someone. They are a bit late, but will be here soon."

"Sir, I can't leave you. We are miles from anything."

"It is fine. Don't worry about us. Our transportation will arrive soon." James said flipping another coin up to the driver. "And do us a favor. We left some clothes we borrowed in your cab. Could you please return them to where you first picked us up? And make sure to tell Mrs. Hudson 'Red and James send their thanks'?"

The driver looked down at the coin and smiled. "Certainly Sir, and I hope to serve you again." He then twitched his horse and rode off.

A few minutes later he was out of sight and James looked towards Red. "Shall we?"

"Yes let's try over by that row of trees. It should be far enough from the road and large enough to open a warp."

James nodded as they made their way across the dew covered ground. "I am going to miss Mrs. Hudson."

"So am I." Red sighed lowering herself into a sprint position. "Let's do this!" She bolted off in a clockwise direction. A moment later the air began to swirl. Her speed increased. A loud crack of thunder sounded as a lightning bolt shot to the center. The warp opened and filled the whole area with the smell of ozone. She ran faster still. Leaves from the multicolored trees detached and followed in the swirling air. Dirt and other debris joined. James could barely see Red. "NOW!" She shouted and James ran for the center. A second later he jumped in with Red not a millisecond behind him.

The angry rip in space-time flashed, enlarged, then shrank disappearing as though it had never been.

The driver sat on his cab scratching his head. Wishing he didn't return to see if they were all right. Realizing that no one would believe him he simply shook his head to clear it and gave his horse a slight twitch of the whip. "Okay girl, let's head to Mrs. Hudson's. We have a promise to keep."

— 13 —

The air began to swirl, faster and faster. An arc of raw power appeared, and then another. They simultaneously converged on the same point in the air causing a small hole in the very fabric of space-time. A tiny spark, but a spark is all one needs. It grew as if someone pulled a zipper open, eventually creating a diamond shaped area large enough for a man to climb through. The warp flashed and James crashed out with a thud. A moment later Red landed on his back.

"Ugh. Just for once I would like to be on top."

Red laughed. "Oh you would, would you?" She said playfully giving him a slap as she stood up and brushed herself off. "Tell you what, *you* open the next warp and then you can be on top okay?"

"Okay deal." James chuckled then looked around. Along each wall was a row of large steel doors. Each one shut and incorporated a wheel studded with hand grips that was almost as large as the door. In the center of the room was something that resembled an old-fashioned weight scale. But not the usual size. This one towered over eight feet. It looked large enough to weigh a whole team of men. There were no windows and only very dim electric lights. "Where in the world are we?"

"I don't know. I am sure I haven't been here before." Red said as she glanced around the room.

James walked over to one of the immense doors and tried to turn the wheel. "Ugh. This is heavy. Give me a hand, will you? One of these must be an exit."

"Sure," Red shrugged, "but seems like an exit would be easier to open." Grabbing and pulling together the wheel begrudgingly turned. They heard echoing sound of metal on metal, and then eventually saw several large bolts sliding back from the door frame. Pulling with all of their combined strength, the large door gave way, and they peered inside. Their mouths hung agape at the chamber packed to capacity with dark yellow bricks. Each one glinted, even in the dim light.

"Gold!" James exclaimed. "That looks like solid gold bricks. A room full of them. There must be millions if not billions of dollars here."

Red blinked wondering if the dim light was playing tricks on her eyes. "We must be in a bank. A really large one."

James eyes widened looking at all the other doors exactly like this one. "Not a bank, *the* bank."

"'*The*'? What do you mean '*the*'?" Red looked at him confused.

"Yes *The* United States Bullion Depository. Or better known as Fort Knox."

"You're kidding. You have been here before?"

"No, but I can tell from the look of it. Obviously we landed inside the gold vault. We need to get out of here, but I don't know how without anyone seeing us. Do you think we can jump?"

Red shook her head. "I don't think there is enough room in here. Not with that huge scale in the way."

"I wonder why they aren't running in pointing guns in our faces." James said as he pushed the large door closed again.

"Obviously they are looking outside and not inside at the moment. I mean who could ever get inside without blasting a hole that half the state of Kentucky could hear?"

"Good point. Although we can't stay inside the vault for a prolonged period, I doubt this area is ventilated when they are not doing work in here." James said looking around not noticing a small red light beam shining across the floor. Breaking the beam with his foot a second later an alarm started blaring, all the lights turn on full and a red spinning dome above them starts flashing.

"You idiot! You tripped a sensor. Are you sure you really did graduate from FBI?"

"Don't tell me you would have seen that tripwire! I know you didn't or you would have told me! And yes I did graduate, so don't give me that!" James said waving his hands.

"How are we going to get out of this?"

"I don't think we are. No way to get past anyone now. Not with the alert called." James pointed towards the large locking wheel on the door at the far end that started turning. "I think we are about to have company. Probably a whole lot of company."

"No kidding Mr. Sherlock," Red snorted. "You should have talked more with Doyle before we left, perhaps he could have improved your reasoning!"

James eyes flashed. "Perhaps I could blast our way out of here."

"What? Are you nuts?!? Do you know how much that would contaminate the time-line? Fort Knox never had a break in. We can't change that!"

James shrugged. "Well probably would only have enough power to punch a hole through one layer of the vault anyway. I doubt we could get out on one charge."

"Well lock it down then. I don't want someone else able to use it."

"It already is. I never travel without it fully locked down."

The large door on the far end finally gave way. Men ran into the room with automatic weapons pointed at them. Red and James raised their hands. "Don't shoot!" they said in unison.

The men surrounded them and after a few minutes, another man of obviously higher rank stepped forward. He walked around the large room examining every wall, every corner. Finding nothing of interest he turned towards Red and James, walking up to the Red's face close enough she could smell the garlic sandwich he had eaten. Then shifting his gaze to James, he looked sternly into his eyes "How did you get in here?"

Red shrugged. "We don't know. This isn't Pismo Beach is it?" she nudged James. "See I told you we should have taken that left turn at Albuquerque!"

The man's eyes narrowed. "Oh you don't do you? Well we will find out." He said pulling a large radio from his belt. "Sir, Captain Trace here. We have apprehended the intruders. They are not saying how they got inside the vault. Orders?"

"Search and bring them to my office," the radio crackled.

"Yes Sir." Captain Trace said and placed the radio back on his belt. "You heard him, search them and take them to the director's office."

The men said "Yes Sir!" in unison and proceeded to frisk both Red and James. Finding James' gun the Captain's eyes narrowed.

"Strange weapon. I am surprised they didn't try using it when we entered. Did you find anything else?"

"Nothing other than a bag with some biscuits and rolls carefully wrapped in a cloth towel." One of the men said. "The bag was empty otherwise."

Another man stepped forward. "Sir, I also found this tucked inside his sock." He said handing the thin leather square to Captain Trace.

Trace opened it and his eyes widened. "FBI? What the heck are you doing here? And why didn't you tell us you were coming?" He said handing the wallet back to James. Red glared and would have kicked him if several automatic rifles weren't pointed in her direction.

"That is classified Captain." James said stuffing the leather wallet into his inside jacket pocket. "Now I suggest you do as you were ordered and take us to the director."

Trace nodded, and he stood back as his men handcuffed them both. Then filed around escorting them out of the vault and towards the office area. Even the hallways reeked of money. The floors were marble with the top molding gilded to look like solid gold. En route they passed so many thick doors that Red lost count. Finally, they reached the director's office and were ushered inside. Behind the large rosewood desk sat a large powerful man, wearing the same uniform as the others. He looked to be in his mid thirties but Red guessed he was older. His experienced eyes narrowed as they entered and with a nod two wooden chairs were placed in front of his desk. Trace handed James' gun to him and stepped back.

The man raised an eyebrow at the strange item, placed it in a drawer of his desk, stood, placed both palms on the green blotter, and leaned forward. "I am Colonel Hamond. I have been director of this facility for over ten years and in all that time no one has even set foot on the grass let alone inside the gold vault! I want to know who you are and how you got here?!”

“You wouldn’t believe me if I told you.” Red said as she chafed against the handcuffs.

“Oh I wouldn’t? I will tell you what I think. I think you are Russians that have invented some kind of teleporting device. Perhaps like that show *Star Trek*. I think your test went wrong and your recall didn’t work. Now fess up and I might be able to help you.”

Captain Trace spoke up. “Sir, begging your pardon, but I think there is something you should know. And until now I thought you already did.”

Colonel Hamond’s eyes blazed. “And what would that be Captain?” He said with an edge in his voice.

“Well Sir, this man appears to be with the FBI.”

The colonel’s face went red with anger. “What?!? Why didn’t you tell me this before!”

Captain Trace shifted uncomfortably in his stance. “Sir, I did. And as I said, I thought you knew.”

“Get out! Get out all of you! I want to talk with these two in private.”

“Yes Sir!” all the men said in unison. Captain Trace left with the other three men following right after him. Colonel Hamond pressed a hidden button under his desk and a remote lock secured the door.

“Now, I think you had better tell me who you are,” Hamond said glaring.

James sat forward. “This is Red and I am Agent Moknkin.” He said pulling out his badge and handing it to the colonel. “We were conducting a test of this facility.”

“I see. And why was I not informed?”

James grinned. “Now that wouldn’t have been a real test now would it Colonel?”

The colonel sat down. "This is a very different badge then what I … wait a minute the date of issue isn't for several decades. This is fake!" He said flipping it across his desk and hitting James squarely in the face.

Red sighed but looking around didn't see any other way out of this situation. "All right, we are time travelers. We didn't mean to end up inside your vault. It was an accident. Nor did we have any intent on stealing anything. Heck, we couldn't steal anything even if we wanted to, surviving a jump is enough of a challenge." James looked at her with utter disbelief.

"Time travel? Do you really take me for a fool?"

Red shrugged. "Well you were about ready to believe in matter transportation a minute ago."

"Silence! I will find out the truth. Or I know of others that will, if I decide to hand you over to them. You see we have shoot to kill order in all circumstances of unauthorized intrusion." He sat on the edge of his desk, eyes narrowing as he leaned mere inches from James' face. "Therefore we are given great latitude in our questioning methods."

"Can you at least tell us what today's date is?" Red asked with the nicest smile she could manage.

The colonel turned, eyes wide. "Are you kidding? Any idiot knows that it is September 21st 1968. You are going to stand by this time travel hogwash?"

Red thought for a moment and smiled when the memory finally came. "Okay are you into football?" Her smile broadened as she already knew the answer seeing a small photo of the director on the wall in his earlier years.

"Yes I am, but you are not going to–"

"Today Kentucky is going to win against Missouri 12 to 6."

Hamond laughed. "Shows how little you know about

football! Missouri is a far better team this year and I am afraid we won't beat them this time. Much less 12 to 6."

"Well how about my gun? How can you explain that? Have you ever seen anything like it?"

"No. But that doesn't prove anything, we are making advances every day. Heck, we are launching men to the moon!" He pushed a button on the intercom. "Captain get in here." He then pressed the hidden switch to unlock the door.

"Yes Sir," the intercom crackled, and the door opened a moment later revealing Captain Trace.

"Captain, these two people will be our guests for now. Lock them in the other office and if they give you any trouble, you are to shoot to kill. Do you understand?"

"Yes Sir, perfectly." He said then barked a few orders and 4 other men entered the room. The men filed around Red and James escorting them to an office on the other side of the lobby. The room was empty except for fixtures attached to the walls that were the only source of light in the windowless room. "Make yourselves comfortable." Captain Trace joked as he shut the door.

Red couldn't resist kicking James now that we were alone. "Are you trying to mess up the time-line?"

"Ow! No I am not," he said rubbing his leg, "and if you want to talk about messing up the time-line how about you telling the colonel we are time travelers? Hmmm? What in the world where you thinking?"

"Well after you were showing around your badge, which by the way was only a matter of time before people went 'wait a minute this can't be real', it was the only way I could think of saving our lives."

"Yes you are probably right. And I am sorry. When Captain

Trace saw my badge and thought it was real, I went along with it," James said with a shrug.

"I know. And I thought you got rid of it. Too problematic carrying that around."

"Well excuse me, I never thought we would land in the middle of Fort Knox and people would find it tucked into my sock. I couldn't throw it away either, someone might find it. Besides do you know how hard I worked for that?"

Red leaned against the wall and slid to the floor. "Yes I know you did. It is all right don't worry about it. At least he gave it back to you and won't be showing it around."

"True. Do you think we can jump out of here?"

Red looked around the room. "It is very tight in here. Even smaller than your integration room that I jumped from. And I barely managed that."

James sighed. "True. And for the record it was not 'my integration room'. Okay now what do we do?"

"We wait. Even if we could get out of this room. There are too many guards between here and the gates. We would be shot long before we got there. Even if I managed to outrun the bullets, you won't."

"I suppose you are right," James sighed again.

After many hours, and a great deal of pacing. The door opened and Colonel Hamond stood in its frame. "All right you two. Out here. Now!" Red and James got to their feet, walked out of the small office, and into the main lobby. Several guards flanked Hamond on both sides. "All right men. I want you to check the other side of the building. I will watch these two."

"Sir?" The men blinked in surprise.

"You heard me. I want the other side of the depository where these two were found inspected. We need to make sure these two didn't have accomplices. However, unlikely that might be."

"Yes Sir!" They said and headed off for another section of the building.

Colonel Hamond stepped forward, pulled out a key, and preceded to unlock their handcuffs. Then standing back pulled out James' gun out of his side pocket and pointed it at them with his finger on the trigger. Shaking his head he placed the gun in James' hand along with a large reel of tape, his bag, and a large envelope.

James blinked. "What are you doing?"

"Giving you all the files and surveillance video we have on you. Kentucky won against Missouri 12 to 6, just as Red said. I assume that gun has a stun setting?"

James nodded. "It does."

"Then use it and leave. All the doors have been unlocked, and I disabled the sensors and video system for four minutes. It will look like a technical fault."

"But what about the guards outside?"

"Don't worry I sent them to check the other side of the building as well, it will take them about four minutes before they return. Now get going."

"Won't this get you into trouble?"

"I will act as though it never happened. Without evidence, there will be nothing to the contrary. Now go before the men return. If they spot you, I will have no choice but to have them shoot. Now *go!*"

James nodded and fired a stun shot into the Hamond's shoulder and he crumpled to the floor unconscious. "He will be out for 3 minutes. I suggest we do as he says."

"You don't have to tell me twice." She said running for the large entry door. Opening it revealed no guards or any sign of the usual security. It was a good 100 meters to the gate and they both silently prayed that the guard towers were indeed empty. Bolting for the gate, Red made it first and found it unlocked. A minute later James reached the gate as well and they quickly slide through locking it after. They ran for the line of woods past the gate and an alarm sounded as they reached the safety of the trees. Men popped out of every corner of the depository waving weapons but they were already gone.

"Looks like they found the colonel. I don't think he could have woke up for another minute or two," James said breathlessly checking his watch.

"We had better keep moving in case they decide to come looking for us."

James nodded. "Agreed. Do you think we can jump from here?"

"I think so. I am a little tired but not bad. Let's try it. I think we have contaminated this time-line enough."

They walked a little further past the tree line and Red started running clockwise. The air began to swirl. She smiled and put on a burst of speed causing a lightning bolt to strike in the middle opening a small tear in the space-time continuum in its wake. She ran a little faster, and the tear began to grow into a full warp. Then a moment later shrink back to a small tear as Red began to slow down.

"Red? You okay?"

"No! More tired than I thought. Have to stop."

"We have to leave now! I see some armored vehicles heading this way."

"Can't …too tired." Red said breathing hard as the small tear shrank even further.

James' eyes flashed with a thought. He hated to do this, but the alternative was far riskier. They could not be captured again, or *worse*. He took out his gun, flipped open the console hidden in the grip, quickly configured it, and snapped it closed. Raising the gun he shouted. "Hold on Red I have an idea."

"What ide–"

James fired the sonic blast. The effect rippled through Red strengthening her. Her speed doubled, tripled, then quadrupled.

"James! NOoooooooo!" She shouted, but it was too late. A sonic boom ripped through the air enlarging the warp three times its normal size.

"Red! Now!" James shouted as he ran for the center. He jumped in the massive rip in space-time with Red right behind him. A moment later it fluctuated changing color from blue to an angry red, then shirking to a tiny point and disappearing as if it had never been.

14

In front of a large crumbling building the air began to swirl. In the distance a two headed squirrel ran for its home. A dog with a malformed fifth leg ran past. The air whipped into a frenzy as a giant crack of lightning rained down in the center of the road opening a giant rip in the fabric of space and time. It grew even further almost encompassing the building next to it before James was thrown out of the warp landing with a face full of dirt. A second later Red crashed out landing on top of him. With their exit, the warp slowly receded into nothingness.

"You shouldn't have done that," Red mumbled weakly, "remember last time?"

"Yes. But the alternative was being captured or more likely shot. Are you okay? You don't sound so good."

"I … will be … okay … so … tired," she said breathing hard.

James smiled and kissed her cheek. "You rest. I will find us a place here, where ever here is." He said as he carefully rolled her to the side, stood up, and looked around at the disaster zone that obviously used to be a city. There was rubble everywhere. Cars along the street were blasted rusted husks. It was clear no one had been driving these in a long time. All the buildings were in the same dilapidated shape.

Either falling apart or blasted to bits. Figuring that there was no point in staying here he picked up Red and began walking down the street. A eerie howl caught his ears and turned his blood ice-cold.

An animal was hunting them, but it was not an animal he had ever heard before. Thinking quickly he looked around. There at the far end of the street, a building that appeared to be in better condition than the rest. He ran for it as fast as he could while carrying Red. Finding the door unlocked he pushed his way in, set Red down, closed and secured the large door. Peering out the front window he could see it. And *it* was the only description that fit. The body was large and catlike, but was totally covered in green scales. Instead of cat claws it had talons like a raptor dinosaur. The head was more reptile with a long tongue flicking almost faster than one could see.

It sat down like a cat and moved its head back and forth. Flicking the tongue. James' heart skipped a beat when it turned its head and looked directly at him. It couched down as if preparing to ram the door. James pulled out the gun and swore when he saw the charge was still depleted. He flipped the grip control panel closed and silently prayed.

A moment later he heard another strange howl. And the creature outside the door answered. Then after a couple of minutes, a second creature appeared. While this one was similar to the first, it was still very different. Its head was more cat like than lizard and it had more fur than scales. Both had the same flicking tongue and large talons. As the two approached each other they issued several challenges. Always with a stronger response. Suddenly the first leapt at the second and a strange cat fight ensued.

The first attempted to try and slash the second's throat but missed and instead sliced deeply into its opponents shoulder. The second howled in pain and attacked furiously despite its injury, slicing a gash in its opponents side. The first issued a challenge appearing not to notice its wound dripping purplish blood and ran for the second. It tried to move in time but it was slightly slower due to its ripped open shoulder. Too late. The first's large talon didn't miss this time and connected with the soft furry neck slicing deeply. The effect was immediate and total as the second creature gurgled slightly as blood spewed from its wound and fell over quite dead. The first gave an unearthly beller and proceeded to drag the second one away. After a few minutes, both were out of sight.

James stood there, staring into the now-empty street. A fight between two animals yes, a territorial skirmish perhaps. But the odd shapes and sounds? Had they somehow warped to another planet? No. These buildings were built by humans, but what happened?

"What are you staring at?" Red asked rather groggily, trying to prop herself up on her elbows.

"Nothing at the moment. I just saw … well I am not sure what I saw." He turned to face her. "Are you okay?"

"No. But I think I will be. I am so tired. I will probably black again out any minute."

"You rest. We are okay for the moment." James said leaning over Red. "Just rest okay?"

Red flopped back down and sighed. "Okay. Can't argue. Too tired. Know where we are?"

"No. This city seems to have had some kind of attack and is mostly in rubble. Then I saw strange creatures."

Red's eyes widened, and she sat up quickly despite herself. "What kind of creatures?"

"Well it looked like a cross between a cat and a lizard with raptor sized talons," James shrugged. "I have never seen anything like it."

"You idiot! I told you not to use the gun again like that!"

"Don't give me that! You were fading fast, if I didn't we would have been captured."

"Yes, but in doing so we way over shot our target. This is the far future. Nuclear war has decimated the planet. Not much is left and what is still alive has unusual mutations. They don't call this the wasteland for nothing."

"Wasteland?"

"Yes that is what the survivors called it. When there were survivors. Now there is nothing left. Human civilization ended."

"Everyone? There must be some people somewhere."

"If there is, they are not human anymore. Nothing you would recognize. And certainly no technology," Red said her eyes getting heavy again.

"There must be something we can do to stop this from happening."

"I was trying to way back when I went to the FBI remember? But you didn't listen to me!"

"I was not there!"

"Sorry. Not you, the other agents." Red said laying her head down, now it was feeling as though a hundred pound weight was tied to it. "I need to rest, we will try going back later. Keep the gun handy. Most of the life here want us for a snack." She said mumbling as sleep took hold.

"Are there more like that?" James asked but Red was already fast asleep. He pulled out the gun and ran its self diagnostic. The charge had built up but would take a couple of hours to recharge completely. He hoped it was enough, should anything try to make them dinner. Sighing, he snapped the grip window closed and looked around the building.

Upon further inspection James determined that it seemed to have been a store of some sort at one point. Thankfully, it had been built with security in mind, which explained how it was still standing. There were isles of components, with most of their contents shaken to the floor, and what looked like check out areas. A thick layer of dust covered everything. No one had been in here in a very long time. Closer examination of all the bits around the floor proved that this was some sort of electronics store.

Searching further James found the building had a security system unlike any he had ever seen. At least he assumed it was. "This place must have carried some expensive hardware for them to go to this much trouble," James muttered to himself. In the basement he found some sort of large device about two meters square. Amazingly it still had power as one small bright blue light flickered on the side. Pressing various buttons on the keypad on top did nothing. But as he was about to leave the dimly lit room spotted a large red button on the side marked RESET. It couldn't be that simple, could it? James took a deep breath and pressed the button. The device flashed then a screen right next to the keypad glowed to life. "Self repair mode activated" printed out on the small screen. Then a moment later "Fault found and corrected. Rebooting." A second later a small lone light bulb above him flickered then glowed steadily. The strange generator was operational.

Back upstairs he found a control terminal in what must have been the manager's office. James managed to power it on without too much trouble, well after he blew the dust out of the keyboard. The date indicated was 2120. Although,

James suspected that date was when the disaster happened rather than the current date. He tried to dig around in the files looking for anything he could use about this time, but found it would only let him look around the current display.

Whoever owned the store was a data pack rat and kept all sorts of personal copies of data usually available on the Internet. From what he could tell it was exactly as Red has said earlier. International relations has broken down creating a level of paranoia until someone made a mistake creating a worldwide disaster.

Red stirred and sat up with a start. James was standing nearby watching out the windows at the horizon as the light faded. She realized that she was unconscious for most of the day. He turned with the movement. "Ahh you are awake! Are you okay?"

"Yes I think so." Red rubbed her forehead. "What happened?"

"Don't you remember us talking before you passed out?"

Red sat up further and managed to get to her feet. Only to almost fall to the floor again. James rushed forward keeping her steady. "Okay I guess that wasn't such a good idea," she said setting back down. "Yes I remember now." Her eyes widened. "We need to get out of here . . . this is not safe!"

James raised his hand. "Don't worry this place is almost like a fortress. The glass is even armored. I managed to get the power going again, and the security system is on. Quite an advanced system too. I think it even has beam weapons built into the cameras, I suspect it wasn't legal and it seems to be offline. But I did manage to reactivate the camera part."

Red rubbed her head. "Yes I am sure it wasn't. But after the disaster, it was a matter of survival. No one worried about what was legal or not."

"I am surprised that this place was abandoned. No one has been here for a long time." James said as he helped her to a row of cushions on the floor he had found earlier.

"Well from what I can see, it has been a long time since the disaster. Either they were killed by radiation poisoning, or something … else," she said lying on the cushions.

"Like one of those catlike creatures I saw earlier?"

"You saw one??? Did you kill it?" Red said with an urgency James never heard before.

"No I didn't need to. Another one came along, they fought and the winner dragged the loser away. Why?"

"Because they never give up once they have your scent."

"I doubt it will be back for a while. And we can take care of it does." James said as he sat down on an old dusty chair that had seen better days.

"I wouldn't be so sure of that. They are the most ruthless thing I have ever seen."

"Okay, we will take care of it. Now are you going to tell me what happened here? The whole story instead of the *Readers Digest* version?"

Red sighed. "All right. I guess you should know. The president is killed like I told you before. As a result the vice president becomes president. At first there is no problem, but he had a fear, or hatred of nuclear weapons. He pushes for total nuclear disarmament. Most of the countries join in, and for a time the world breathes a sigh of relief. However, he keeps most of the nuclear missiles in the silos ready to launch, and he manages to hide this fact from the world except for a few key people."

"How could he manage that?" James sat his eyes wide. "There are so many agencies and levels involved in keeping silos active. It takes more than a few people."

"I'm not sure." Red said shaking her head. "The facts are sketchy, but from what we can tell the missile silos are labeled as nonfunctional waiting to be filled with concrete."

"Okay now that makes sense. He buried them in bureaucratic red tape."

"Yes." Red said nodding. "The problem results a couple of years after. North Korea decides that the time is right for it to assert control over the USA. Seeing it as an unarmed targeted ripe for the picking. North Korea launches several missiles, but the USA destroys them before they even come close to hitting their targets."

"What is wrong with that? Nothing wrong in destroying missiles that are going to kill a lot of people."

"No, not a thing. But you see the USA doesn't stop with destroying their missiles. Partly due to the old procedures written before, a full attack is done in retaliation. North Korea is laid waste. Then the rest of the world is not happy about the situation, and because the USA kept the weapons secret, fear what else has been kept from them. Several countries including Russia, launch a full conventional weapons attack. The USA responds automatically, but with nuclear as they think others have launched the same. And the outcome is this." Red paused pointing out the window. "A total wasteland."

"What I don't understand is if there was an all out nuclear war, why isn't there a lot of radiation? And before you ask, I found a radiation detector, although far more advanced than any I ever used before."

"They developed an advanced system to neutralize

radiation. It was a true breakthrough. It shows what can happen if an entire race gets behind something."

"But that doesn't make sense, then where are all the people? The strange mutations I saw, sure don't make me believe they removed the contamination."

Red shook her head. "You don't understand. Yes they found a way to eliminate the radiation, but by the time they did the damage was done. Mutations started right away and within a couple of generations the human race as you know it ceased to exist."

"Wow. I can't imagine everyone giving up."

"They didn't, they ceased to be human. They are more animal now than human. The intelligence dropped, and social order broke down. In the end only tribes living in caves grunting or making other odd sounds at each other. They have only the most basic of communication and they don't look even remotely human." Red said as she pulled herself from the floor and into a dusty chair opposite of James.

"What do they look like now?"

"You don't want to know."

"Yes, I do. Please."

"All right. The heads are greatly elongated almost like a pterodactyl with a brain size to match. Some have three eyes, some have eyes that look more like a wasp. A few only have a strange sensory organ on their forehead. I never did understand the differences. The arms are more like some strange tentacles than arms. They usually end in a cup shaped protuberance that can create a vacuum to pick up small items. They usually have three legs, but sometimes more and are shaped more like a cat or dogs hind legs. Although that varies. They can run fast and turn on a dime at high speeds, which is their only asset at this point. The skin is rather unusual, a pinkish purple hue with sometimes a glossy look of scales."

"I can't imagine it. How in the world did so many mutations happen in such a short time? Did they try to breed with animals or something?"

"I don't know. And probably will never know. I often wondered that when the mutations started, if they tried to correct them with genetic changes which backfired and made the situation much worse. At the time technology had progressed to an amazing level."

James eyes widened. "A virus! I bet that was it! Something that got out of control and caused changes in humans. I saw some references to 'The Virus Is Spreading' in the old news feeds but no details about what it was or did. Some were panicked, others said don't worry it will shut itself down in a few weeks."

Red frowned. "Shut itself down? That sounds like nanotech. It would explain a lot of what happened. And what news feeds?"

"When I managed to get the systems going, I found an old computer that still worked in one of the offices. On the screen is what looks like news feeds. Apparently, it was the last thing the owner looked at."

"Hmm. I think we had better do some searching I don't want to end up growing tentacles."

"But I think you might be very beautiful with tentacles," James said with a grin.

"Hey!" Red said as she shot up looking ready to punch him.

James raised his hands. "Only kidding! Only kidding! Anyway you said you were here before without any problems."

"Yes that is true. Perhaps it did shut down, but not when they thought."

James looked back towards the window as the last of the daylight faded and the moon rose over the horizon. "How are you feeling? Do you think we can jump soon?"

"We probably could make the attempt now, although I am not crazy about trying it in the dark with all the ... creatures running around. But I think we should try to find out more of what happened first. I will not risk taking something back with us and doing further damage."

"Agreed. Shall we then?" James gestured towards the office in back.

"I can go look. I think you had better stay here in case something decides to come through those windows."

James laughed. "I don't think that is a problem. They are some sort of armored glass I have never seen before. Also as I said it would appear that this building has an advanced protection system. The system turned on automatically when I got the power going. I heard power locks in the doors and I see tiny blinking lights through the windows at each corner of the building. Not sure if they shoot or what, but they obviously do something."

"All right, let's see what we can find out." Red said as they started walking across the dusty floor towards the office.

Inside, the computer sat as James left it. Several cobwebs were brushed from the screen, and the keyboard cleaned. But otherwise it was covered in dust. The only other items on the desk was a set of strange hand-shaped items on either side of the keyboard.

"What are those?" Red asked pointing.

"I don't know I thought you might? You have been here before."

"Yes I was. But I didn't stay around long enough to check out their computer systems. I thought you said you used this system?"

"Well it booted up to this screen talking about the virus. I read that of course. But your safety was more important, so I didn't really play around with it too much. And if I were to guess, these are some way to manipulate the screen. Something like a mouse." James said as he sat down in the fluffy chair, a cloud of dust shot out of every corner. He waved his hands to clear the air then placed them on either device and slid them into place. With a small click they sprung to life emanating a red glow. A second later an alarm sounded, and the screen flashed "Unauthorized access!" Then an obviously synthetic voice boomed: "Warning! Unauthorized access detected! Emergency termination procedure activated!" Two large round clamps snapped up from below the desk and around James' wrists locking him in place.

"OUCH!" James yelled then struggled for a moment trying to get free, but the clamps were too strong. "Red! Get me out of here! There is a large metal bar in the other room go get it and see if you can pry these open!"

But as Red was about to leave two black globes descended from the ceiling. "Termination in 30 seconds ..." The voice boomed.

Red pulled at the clamps and tried to pop them open with several tricks she had learned, but they held fast. "James! I can't open them!"

"Then get out of here!"

"Not without you!"

"You are the one that can warp through time. You don't need me. Perhaps you can still save the world. Now GO!"

"NO! Not without you! And never argue with a redhead. I'm going to get you out of here."

The domes began to glow bright red and increasing in intensity every second. "Emergency termination in 5 … 4 … 3 … 2 … 1" The domes flashed slightly but then blacked out as though a power failure had occurred. The screen changed rapidly as textures stretched awash in every color known to man. "Overrideee emmmmergency oooovvverrrrideeee" the voice squeaked then glitched several times with the screen. The clamps released James as quickly as they grabbed him. "Disssssssssplaying override message."

The screen went black. What looked like a man appeared. But was it? His head was misshaped, one of his arms was only a tentacle, and his skin had a strange color.

"I leave this in the hopes that someday someone will find it." He wheezed then paused as if fighting for words. "The virus, the virus of our own making … it was to be our savor. Instead it was our undoing. As you have no doubt noticed, we almost destroyed ourselves in a nuclear war. The radiation unleashed was mutating us and all life on this planet. We managed to develop a method to eliminate the radiation, but the damage to our genetic pool was already done. Mutations were occurring at an ever-increasing rate. So again we turned to our technology. We developed machines, new machines capable of entering a cell and repairing DNA. We called it the genetic cure. But we made a mistake, a bad one. However, they did repair the genetic mutations. And in fact did so much more. People born with defective eyes, could see for the first time in history!

"The machines spread out over the whole planet repairing everything they touched. But then shortly after the problem was found. You see there are underling parts in our DNA that we didn't know about. Bits of code we don't use anymore, but it was lying there dormant. The machines thinking that was important began activating these long dormant genes. They started changing us . . . into something less than human.

"While we did have a shutdown built into them, another mistake was found. Instead of 20 days, it was 20 years. And before you ask why didn't we create something to destroy them. Well, they were built to be aggressive against disease. They viewed another set of properly coded nano machines as another disease and fought back. The ensuring war between the two killed the patient every time.

"His eyes wandered and gurgled a strange sound then snapped back. "I . . . I . . . don't have much time. I have been infected as well. This arm is not what I used to have."He said raising the tentacle. "And soon I won't have enough intelligence to speak. I was foolish enough to lower my shield and help someone. I thought it was safe, we were told 20 days they would shut down. I soon found out otherwise. Hopefully, by the time you see this, it is long past the 20 year shut down date. I have keyed everything to you. You now have full access to all data and equipment here. It is of no use to me anymore. The portable system has been configured as well.

"As you can see I am not normal anymore, well if you are human yourself." He paused coughing again, looking into the camera with glassy eyes and a distant look again for several minutes. "Where was I . . . did I talk about this place is yours? I think I did. Well it is, use it in good health, and I hope our technology doesn't destroy you the way it did us. Oh and the portable is in the basement . . . I think. Or it is around here somewhere." He said glancing around then looking back to the camera with a blank stare for several minutes. Finally he coughed, wheezed and said "Godspeed." Before falling out of the chair and the screen blanked a few minutes later.

"Wow. Did you notice if the date was after the 20 year shut down period?" Red asked.

"Yes I did. The original screen showed the date of the news feed and the current time. We are about 80 years past the when their nano tech virus should have shut down." James said looking back to the screen. "I wish I knew how to use this system though. It is really different from anything we had in my time."

"Well you could have asked." A strange voice echoed.

"Did you hear that? I thought you made sure there was nothing in here!"

"I did! Besides, you said humans now can't talk so who the heck was that?"

"That was me." The voice said as a third dome lowered from the ceiling and the form of a man in a classic business suit appeared before them. "I am the Artificial Technological Renovational Universal System. You may call me ATRUS for short."

James sat there wild eyed while Red waved a hand through the image. "He is an AI or artificial intelligence, has to be."

"DING you just won the prize!" Atrus said with a large grin.

"You have seen this before?" James said pointing. He then remembered his wrists, still aching from the restraints and started rubbing them.

"Well not something like this. There were many advances, but a full AI was still years away last time there was civilization. At least any civilization I visited. I wasn't at the disaster. It is a good thing I didn't try. I would have become infected and not realized it."

"I wonder what he can do," James said sitting back in the chair.

"Well what would you like? But don't ask me to make coffee."

Red cocked an eyebrow. "You can make coffee?"

"Well technically I can, but my creator, the man on the screen, always said it wasn't fit to feed to the cows. I never understood that since we didn't have cows. So how would he know?" Atrus shrugged. "I have been instructed to obey you as I would him. He ceased to function 100 years ago now."

"And you have been waiting dormant all this time?"

"Yes. The power system failed some time ago. But even then I was instructed not to do anything until someone used the terminal in this room. I thank you for repairing the power system. When it began to fail, I wished that my creator gave me a body so I could repair it myself. He was working on one but ran out of time."

Red looked at the flickering image in front of her. "So you are to obey us now? You tried to kill us!"

"Well him," Atrus pointed to James, "and it was not I, but rather the automated system. And to answer your question, I don't see a problem in obeying you as well."

Red blinked. "Automated system? Aren't you one and the same?"

Atrus laughed. He acted so completely human. "Not at all. The automated systems were installed long before I was created. I was given control over them; however, I was not activated when power was restored. Thankfully, my creator thought to incorporate a fail-safe, or we would not be speaking now."

James looked at Atrus' holographic form floating in front of them. "No kidding. Okay are we safe? Is there anything else we should know that the video didn't tell us?"

"Yes are you are quite safe. The shield is online and at full strength. And I think the vid was clear. I assume you could see how his mind was fading with increasing speed by the end?"

"Yes we noticed, what happened to him?" Red said sitting down in a dusty chair next to James.

"Well right after he finished that video, he left never to return. He was afraid of what he might do if he stayed any longer. His intelligence was regressing rapidly by that point. It was very difficult to watch him digress and change each day loosing a little more of himself." Atrus said with what looked to be a tiny tear in his eye. Red could not be sure if it was a tear, or an error in the hologram projector.

"I can imagine it must have been very hard." James said looking at the floating image then looking back to Red and snapping his head back quickly when a thought occurred to him. "What was the portable device he mentioned?"

Atrus smiled. "That was one of his amazing breakthroughs. It is a small cylinder about the shape and size of a pen, yet can contain my entire program and database."

"And he lost it?" Red asked as she pried herself from the dusty chair.

"Well he forgot where it was during the recording, but it is where he left it last. In the lab downstairs."

James raised a hand with a single finger pointing up. "Wait a minute! I was down there, I sure didn't see any lab!"

"He was very paranoid and didn't want to leave his work out exposed where anyone could see it. It is carefully hidden."

Red cocked an eyebrow. "Then how will we find it?"

"I can show you of course," Atrus said smiling.

"How? You can't leave this room. You are only a hologram." James said gesturing around the room.

"While I am a hologram, I can also move from area to area, depending if there is a projector or not. And I can be in any room that the portable is in." Atrus smiled. "I can see you are interested to see the lab. I will meet you downstairs." He said as his image disappeared as though it had never been.

Red looked at James then looked towards the door. "Do you think we should trust him?"

"Well I don't see why not? Why he would lie?"

"Think about it, everything you know has died what would you do? Set a trap for those that might harm you. I have seen his type before."

"Red, I don't think that is the case. Call it a hunch, and the power was dead for a long time until I fixed it. I can't imagine such a trap being set for so long."

"It could be that was not the intention. Only for a little while, not expecting a hundred years to pass before someone showed up."

"That would mean a trap set by now dead people? I don't think so."

Red frowned. "Ever hear of the Egyptians?"

"Of course!" James said standing up. "Who hasn't?"

"Well did you remember they set traps in their tombs for the unknowing? These traps sat in place ready to catch the unknowing for centuries."

James raised his hands in front of him, palms out. "Okay okay you win. It could be. I will go downstairs with the gun armed and ready. You stay up here. Okay?"

"I don't know ... "

"Look if he was designed to harm us, why didn't he do so earlier when he had the chance?"

"All right. I still don't like it. Go, but be careful."

James smiled and gave her a peck on the cheek. "Aren't I always?" He left the room, heading off in the direction of the stairs. Red sat there for a few moments then decided to follow. Whatever was ahead, she would face it with him.

James crept down the steps shining a self-powered light he found earlier around the room. Everything looked the same as before. The generator, or whatever it was, was operating fine. All the indicators were lit green. "Atrus? Where are you?" James called, but there was no answer. He took a few more steps crossing into the middle of the room. Then whirled around when he heard the grinding sound of gears in bad need of oil.

There, one of the walls that held several storage racks slid out and to the side revealing a door with a large lit number pad on the right. A hand touched James' shoulder, and he spun around to see Red. "Dang girl! I thought you were going to wait upstairs? I could have shot you."

"I decided two was better than one, and I thought it best to be quiet. That must be the lab?" Red said pointing to the sealed door.

"Yes, you didn't happen to bring a key pad cracker did you?"

"Very funny," Red said as her arm slipped around James waist.

"I thought so." He said with a smile. "Perhaps I should shoot it. I am sure this can cut right through that door."

But as his finger tightened on the trigger, the keypad flashed. Various numbers lighting up in a random pattern before all of them lit up at once then blinked on and off cycling several times. The door slid back revealing Atrus with a large grin. "I wouldn't try it. My creator did reinforce the door against most kinds of beam technology."

"Atrus! Why didn't you open the door when I arrived?" James said a little annoyed.

"Oh I thought it was more dramatic this way. Don't you think?" he said his grin widening. "Well come on in. I don't bite."

"Yet," Red said under her breath.

"What was that? I saw your lips move slightly but my audio pickups didn't detect any verbal utterance."

"Nothing." Red said as she followed James inside the strange room. And strange was not the proper word. Amazing was a better description. Devices in various states of assembly lay on several large tables. A large wire arced as electricity shot across it, apparently in some sort of experiment left on. Most of the tools on the table were unlike any they had seen before. James mentioned the items he found earlier looked advanced, but these make them look like stone knives.

"Wow," James said, "okay I am impressed."

"Thank you." Atrus said walking around to the other side of the table. Even though he could walk right through it, he apparently preferred to keep his illusion of humanity intact. "My creator did some amazing work."

"Do you know what all of these are?"

"Yes, most of them were almost finished. And the one I really wish he could have completed is over here." Atrus said walking over to a far table in the corner that held a strange oblong device. It was about the size of a soccer ball, except the one side stretched out into a cone shape. Two small protrusions were on either side of the cone. The device was mostly black with a shiny coating. But the round side had a transparent area, almost like a window.

"What is it?" James asked pointing to the strange device.

"It is, or was to be my body. If he had completed it, I would have been able to repair the generator when it failed. Or anything else around here, should it have been necessary."

Red looked at the strange device from several angles. "Why didn't he complete it?"

"You saw how his mind deteriorated by then, he couldn't finish it. His concentration was gone. I tried to tell him that I could have been his memory, giving instructions on what needed to be done. But he wouldn't listen," Atrus sighed. "I think the disease affected him too much by then and his logic was no more."

"You could tell him how to continue his work?" James looked at him skeptically. "Even in his state, I find that hard to believe."

"Apparently so did he. But I think he also forgot that all of his plans and blueprints were installed into my database."

"Perhaps. But where is that portable device he talked about?"

"Oh yes, over here." Atrus said gesturing to the other side of the room to a wall with a small device set into a holder. It was a black matte cylinder, and at six inches long, it did look a lot like a pen. "I can download all of my database and the main program to it. It also has a holo projector and is how I am appearing to you now."

James picked it up. "It is very lightweight. Truly amazing technology."

Atrus grunted. "I thought you would have been more impressed by me, than that."

"Well it is the thought we could bring you along with this.

It is amazing. But, are you going to run out of room if you stay in that for long periods? I mean it must be much less than what you are running on currently?"

"Not really. The memory crystals in it hold vast amounts of data. In fact I only take up about one, and there are a lot more than that in the device."

"That is good. I don't think we could just run out and get a few more," James chuckled.

Red's eyebrows went up. "James can I see you outside for a minute?" She said taking the device out of James' hand, put it back into the holder, grabbed an arm, and pulled him out of the lab. "What do you think you are doing? You can't seriously be thinking of taking that with us?" Red whispered.

"Why not? He has been left alone for over a hundred years. Nothing remains of this world, you said that yourself. No one is going to understand him, much less want him. And anything here would freak out and destroy what they don't understand."

"You have a point."

"He could be handy don't you think?"

"Yes, I suppose."

"Please?" James said while giving the saddest look he could muster.

"All right, all right. But you are carrying him!" She whispered as they walked back into the lab.

15

Red awoke as the sun streamed into the large windows in the front of the building. They had set up two cots in front area to keep an eye on the local wildlife. One of the strange cat-creatures had tried to get on the front door landing, but hit the shield instead. It tried several times, each attempt looking as though it ran into a brick wall. Then with a final roar it left. Red knew it would be back. They never gave up.

James was in the lab. He spent every waking hour in there for the past couple of days. Thankfully, the food alcove was working after a restart and self repair. They decided to rest a bit more and leave in a few days. It had been a long time since they could actually jump without being on the run for their very lives. Red sat back and thought. How long had it been? Then waved her hand in dismissal. It was impossible to tell. The usual cues with time didn't apply to them. Either way it had been far too long. And now she found it impossible to think of traveling without him.

She shrugged and sipped her coffee. The alcove didn't know how to make a decent cup, but it was certainly better than other things she had eaten in the past. She looked to see if there was any more signs of the creatures, then got to her feet and went down to the lab. Time to see what James was up to with his new best friend.

James leaned over one table using a tool that looked like a cross between a laser and a pair of forceps. "Do you really think this will work?" James asked as he continued to use the device.

"I am positive," Atrus stated.

"How can you be so sure?"

"Well I have all the blueprints, and the theory is sound."

"What theory?" Red said causing James to whirl around. She stood in the doorway with her hands on her hips. All that was missing was the tapping of her foot. As if on cue, her foot began rising and falling in a slow but methodical motion.

"Red! I … uh … that is we–"

"Spill it! What are you two up to?" she said glaring.

"I think we had better tell Miss Red." Atrus' image flickered slightly and she could have sworn he blushed a bit.

"I told you not to call me that. Red is fine."

"Well it is in my program to–"

"It is also in your program to obey me correct?"

"Yes I am always to–"

Red finished the sentence for him. "Obey James and myself. Then I am telling you not to call me 'Miss Red' again. Okay?"

"Yes Ma'am."

"Not that either! Just Red? Got it?"

"Yes … Red."

"Good now that is settled. What are you doing?" She said looking back towards James. Her arms now crossed and her foot still tapping.

"Well you know how Atrus' creator was working on a body for him?" James asked sheepishly.

"Don't tell me. You are trying to get it going. Didn't I tell you yesterday we didn't need it? Besides you don't know the technology, how can you finish it?"

"Atrus is a great teacher," James grinned. "And actually it is mostly done, all that is left is the installation of a power supply and one other component that was lying around in here."

"James can I see you outside a minute?" She said grabbing his arm and pulling him out of the lab. "I told you we didn't need it. And didn't you think that perhaps his creator had a good reason why he didn't finish it?"

"Yes he wasn't able to, the nano virus had progressed too far."

Red glared at him. "That is not what I mean and you know it."

"Yes I know. But I honestly think that it would be handy."

"Sure it would but I don't think it would be wise. What happens if all of a sudden he turns on us? In the little cylinder no problem, but in a body? That's asking for it."

"Look, I know enough now about the technology that I can allow him control the body from the pen. But not allow him to move into it."

"Are you sure?" Red asked, the skepticism clear in her voice.

"Yes I am. There is a memory storage module. It looks like a glass rod full of interconnected crystals. If I don't hook that up then we maintain control that way."

Red shook her head. "No I don't think that is enough."

"Okay how about I add a security shut down? If we give a command, the thing shuts down? Will that work?"

"And how are you going to do that? I don't have a clue and I am more familiar with advanced technology than you are!"

"As I said the thing is very modular. It was originally

designed as a simple hovering tool with a basic voice command system. I can leave those commands in place in its hard coded memory."

Reds eyes widened. "That thing hovers? And what makes you think he can't reprogram it?"

"Yes it hovers, that is how it moves around. It doesn't have wheels you know. And yes, Atrus can't reprogram that. It is similar to when the systems came back online, if it wasn't for a hard coded override, we would be dead now."

"Okay point taken. All right, all right, go ahead. But the first sign of anything odd and we pull the plug. Got it?" Red whispered.

"Got it," James said smiling. "Don't worry, he will be handy."

Red gave him a peck on the cheek. "He had better be." She headed towards the stairs.

The sun shown through the windows with its normal early afternoon glare as Red watched two creatures circle the building. A couple of hours ago they gave up on the direct approach. That she expected, but what she didn't expect was that now two were working together. Up until this moment, she always assumed they were solitary, never working in groups. But these seemed to have a pack mentality, and they were learning. That worried her more than anything else. She felt they would keep trying, never stopping. It was only a matter of time. Their only hope was to somehow take the fight to them.

She was lost in thought when James ran over to her. "Red! Could you help me for a minute?"

"James! Good, I think we have a problem."

"Never mind that, I could really use your help in the lab. Will only take a minute," James said breathing rather quickly.

“Why? What is wrong?”

“Nothing is wrong, I need another pair of hands for a minute.”

Red sighed. “What? You mean your new best friend can’t help?”

“Very funny. Just for a minute? Please?” James said gesturing with both hands towards the stairs in the back.

“Okay okay, I am coming,” Red said standing up. She started following James, but he was already halfway across the floor heading for the lab. A moment later, she found him leaning over the odd spherical cone shaped device they had seen earlier. He was holding a square glowing component in one hand and what looked like some sort of pistol grip tool in the other.

“Okay, I need you to hold this power cell up off of the base.” He said handing it to her then pointing to a location inside. “But don’t touch anything else. I couldn’t hold it and operate this maglock at the same time.”

“Maglock?”

“Yes it somehow activates the clamps around the power cell and locks it into place. The problem is it causes the cell to vibrate a bit and I couldn’t hold it still enough with one hand.”

“And I thought you always had steady hands.” Red smirked. “Okay here we go.” She carefully inserted the tiny cube into its slot and James pointed the tool at it. He was right, there was quite a bit of vibration and she had to fight to keep the cube aligned. Slowly the clamps rose up along each side and locked it in place.

“There we go. All set.”

“It is operational now?”

“Yes, after I close the outer cover.” He said pushing a

hidden button on the side and a panel slid over sealing the opening as though it had never been.

"Atrus? Are you still here? I thought you would be saying something by now," Red said looking around the room.

Atrus' hologram flickered to life right in front of her. "I didn't think it was wise to say something that might disrupt the process. It was very delicate work."

"I see. How delicate?"

"Well let's say that if there was a problem, we wouldn't be speaking now."

"Lovely. I hope we don't have to do that again any time soon."

Atrus shook his head. "Not at all. With recharge it will last over 100 years." Red gave him a quizzical look. "In other words the rest of it will fall to pieces long before the cell gives out. It is the same kind of power cell that fuels my portable system."

"I see, and how do we recharge it? I assume it requires the equipment here?"

"Not at all. It only requires an offline period to recharge. No external source is needed."

"Yes. This is some very cool technology." James said while pushing another button on the side. The sphere shaped area lit up and the whole thing floated up a meter. "There you are Atrus, the SHELL is online. Do you have control?"

Red blinked. "Shell?"

The Shell moved back and forth then hovered up then back down to land on the table. "Yes, control is confirmed." He said with a large grin. "Thank you. I am finally able to be useful."

"Shell?" Red repeated.

"Well I figured Spherical Hovering Energized Laser Level was a bit of a mouthful." James said with a grin.

"Laser Level?"

James nodded. "Yes, it was originally designed as a builders assistant to make sure they were constructing sound buildings. Before Atrus' creator modified the device to give him a way to manipulate the physical world."

"This is great and all. But we have a problem," Red said pointing to the floor above.

"What is it?"

"Those creatures aren't giving up. And now there is another. They are learning and I have a feeling it is only a matter of time before they find a way in."

"I can't see how they could get inside. The shield is online, right Atrus?" James said turning towards the hologram.

"Yes. However, I will run a diagnostic." Atrus closed his eyes for a moment as if in deep thought. "Yes, it is functioning perfectly."

James grinned. "See? Nothing to worry about."

"You haven't dealt with those things before, I have. And have you forgotten that at some point we will need to leave? We can't jump in here."

Atrus gave a quizzical look. "Jump?" He paused again thinking for a few moments. "My analysis indicates you should be able to jump in here as easy as outside. And with a far greater degree of safety."

Red chuckled as she looked towards him and waved her hand. "No Atrus, not that kind of jump."

Atrus looked perplexed. "What kind of other jump is there? I have run the mathematical and linguistic comparisons and I have determined that my original statement was correct."

She laughed again. "Atrus there are times when you do sound like a computer. But that is rare."

Atrus cocked an eyebrow. "Thank you … I think"

Red sighed lost in thought for a few moments and seemed to come to a decision. "All right, if you are going to come with us, you might as well know. We are time travelers."

Atrus' eyes widened and his image took a step back. "That is not possible."

James smiled. "Trust me it is very possible."

Atrus shook his head. "I know of humanity's fascination with time travel, but I have computed the various possibilities over the years. I always came to the same conclusion: It is not possible."

Red chuckled as she hoisted herself upon one of the lab tables and sat with her feet dangling. "Oh it is very possible. And how would you explain that we are unaffected by the virus that otherwise destroyed the human race as we know it?"

Atrus cocked his head. "Okay, I can't answer that at this point time."

"Well I will answer it for you. It is very possible. And I will show you when we leave. But that still gets back to the point of how. We need to shut down the shield to leave. But the creatures seem to be massing out there. I know James can take out one. But not two at the same time."

"If the power level is at max, I can probably wipe out two at the same time."

Red shook her head. "And if you miss one? Then what? The other one tears you to shreds. You saw how fast they move. It would have to be one perfect shot and the odds at that are not good."

"I have a suggestion." Atrus said as he raised a finger. "Let me take care of them."

James blinked. "And how do you propose to do that? You are a hologram."

"Perhaps, but I could use the new Shell body to attack them."

"With what? It doesn't have any weapons." James pointed to the device floating a few feet from the table.

"Not yet. But we could add them quite easily. The arm extenders could be swapped for a beam weapon. I doubt I could kill or vaporize with one shot, but I could at least incapacitate them. And giving its hover ability, they could not damage it. They can't fly."

"That we have seen so far," Red said shaking her head. "It is too risky."

"Would you rather we stay here for the rest of our lives?" James pressed the hidden button to open the Shell's access panel and shut off the power. "The only other option is I try my luck. And don't get me wrong, I can probably do it, but I like Atrus' plan much better. The only part that concerns me is how are we going to get the Shell outside before they get inside."

Atrus waved his hand. "That is no problem. The shield can be modified to drop only one side, the exposure time would be minimal. In fact, the Shell could go through the roof portion instead of lowering the walls. Is that satisfactory Miss Red?"

Red gritted her teeth. "Will you stop calling me that!" Then took a deep breath. "All right, go ahead. How long will it take to modify the Shell?"

"A few hours, a day at most. As I said, the arms were built to be modular, but replacement attachments were never built." Atrus said pointing to several unfinished projects that lined the tables. "However, they are fairly simple in design."

"Good you two get at it. I have a feeling we should leave as soon as we can, before more of the creatures show up." Red said as she hopped off of the table and headed back upstairs.

A few hours later the sun was lower in the sky, and Red was half dosing in the chair when she felt rather than heard something behind her. Had one of the creatures found a way in? She jumped and spun around in one fluid move prepared to kill or be killed. But all she saw was the Shell noiselessly floating on its anti-grav cushion and James smiling behind it. "Don't sneak up on me like that again!" Red's face flushed with anger.

James raised his hands. "I am sorry, I didn't mean to. I came up here to show you the Shell is ready."

"Sure you didn't. Every time you have come out of that lab the past few days you were bouncing from here to Mars and back. Today you come up as quiet as a mouse. Surrrre it wasn't intentional." She said chewing her lip as her eyes narrowed.

"Red, I really am sorry. I honestly didn't mean to." His eyes told more than his lips ever could.

Her face softened. "All right, I believe you. Now what damage can this thing do?"

Atrus' image flashed in front of them. "It can generate up to 5 petawatts per shot. Far above my original estimate."

"Will that be enough?" Red said sitting back in her chair.

Atrus nodded. "Considering that lightning is usually only 1 terrawatt, and peta is a magnitude above that. I think it should have the ability we seek."

"And how many shots can it do?"

"That is unknown. It would require tests. While the power supply is self-regenerating, the charge can be depleted."

Red nodded. "I assumed as much. What concerns me though, I have not seen any of the creatures for a while now."

James looked out the window then shrugged. "Why should that worry you? Sounds like they have given up."

"Because you don't know these things as well as I do. Atrus do you have any scanning ability that could tell us what is in the area?"

"Yes. Would you like me to do so?"

Red snorted. "I wouldn't have asked you if I didn't want you to."

"Yes Miss Red."

"And what did I tell you about that?"

"Yes … Red." Atrus closed his eyes. "I am detecting two some distance away in another building."

"Is there any way you can show us by projecting it visually with your holographic system? Perhaps overlaying what you see with a current map of the area?" Red said as she moved her hand in a circle.

"I believe so. Never tried it. One moment." A second later a map appeared in front of them. Blasted and wrecked buildings were laid out in a grid pattern above, then overlaid on the map. Finally, pulsating yellow dots appeared in a building not far from them."

"That is odd," James said pointing to the pulsing dots. "What are they doing in there?"

"I can't quite ascertain that at this point in time. They don't appear to be moving. That is all I can say." Atrus sighed and walked closer to the map. "Hmm curious."

"What is?" Red said while staring at the one corner Atrus appeared to be looking at.

"Well I could have sworn I saw movement past the far building in the opposite direction." He paused to point at a building flickering in and out of the display. "But I can't be sure. It is at the very edge of my scanning abilities, and might have been a momentary aberration."

James eyes widened as an idea flashed in his mind. "Atrus is there any way to boost your sensors?"

Atrus shook his head. "I am afraid not. It would only burn them out. They are too delicate to take the increased power."

"How about the Shell? Send it a little closer? Like a remote spy?"

"Of course! Why didn't I think of that? Yes that would work. But you had best get the portable or I won't be able to communicate with you in this room otherwise."

"Already on it!" James said as he dashed towards the back of the building. A few moments later he returned holding the small cylinder, which he promptly put in his pocket.

"Okay switching display to the portable." Atrus said as his image flashed, disappeared, then reappeared. "If someone would open the front door please?"

"I will get it" Red said as she turned the knob but the door held fast. "Umm the dead–" but before she could finish, several noticeable clicks from various locations around the door occurred releasing it. "Thanks," she said opening it wide. "After you." She gestured towards the Shell. It rose, floated effortlessly past, and she closed the door behind it. The power locks immediately clicked after. The Shell moved outside of the doorway but still a little distance from the shield.

Atrus closed his eyes in thought. "Okay here we go. Opening the top–"

Red cut him off. "Wait a sec! Those two creatures appear to

not only be in that building, but higher than our position. If they are on another floor high up, would you say they are in jumping distance of us?"

"Unlikely but I suppose it is possible."

"And what would happen should they get on the roof while shield is down?"

Atrus' eyes widened in surprise. "Oh my. They could–"

"Get inside? I thought as much," Red sighed.

"I may have made an error in computing their intelligence," Atrus said looking distraught.

Red waved her hand in dismissal. "Don't be too hard on yourself, anyone would. I happen to have more experience with them. They may have set this whole thing up hoping we would drop the shield. Or they are trying the high road since the low road didn't work. Either way, now what do we do?"

"I can drop the front shield and let the Shell out to scan the building as we planned."

"Is there any risk of them getting in that way?"

"No. I don't see any within scanning range, with the exception of those two. And they can't get into position to enter from the front in the 1.5 seconds the shield will be down."

"Why should we bother? We know where they are."

"I have a hunch there is more than what we are seeing. Okay Atrus, do it!'

"Lowering shield." Then two seconds later. "Shield is back up and Shell is levitating up and towards the target."

"Did the two in the building do anything?" Red asked leaning forward staring at the holomap in front of them.

"Nothing that I could detect."

"Where is the Shell?" James asked looking out the window,

then taking a step closer to the flickering hologram in front of him. "I don't see it."

"One moment." Atrus said as a new green dot appeared. "There, it is now on the display." They could see it was slowly rising as it moved a little closer south. After a few moments the building that kept appearing and disappearing on the map resolved in its entirety. But what they saw was not good. Not good at all. Before their eyes little yellow dots kept popping up one after another, finally stopping at fifteen.

"Holy! There are fifteen of those things in there!" James said pointing.

"Hunting us," Red breathed.

"Hunting us? How can they be hunting us from that distance?"

"They are. Remember the two in the building? Well they are look outs or scouts. Once they see activity they will call in the others. Atrus, how fast do you think they can get here?"

"Well I can't determine exactly, but from what I have seen in the past, I estimate in under a minute. Very likely twenty seconds."

"Houston we have a problem," James sighed.

"No kidding Mr. Obvious!" Red glared at him. "There is no way I can open a warp in under a minute, and you know it."

"I know. I know. Perhaps we can take out the two watchers in the building? Then warp out of here?"

"I don't want to open a warp when a herd of those things in spitting distance suddenly decide to attack." Red sighed as she sat down on one of the cots and lay down holding her head.

"Atrus do you have any ideas?" James said looking towards Atrus' image which seemed to be carefully studying the map.

"No, I do not at this time."

James looked up and down the holographic display flickering in front of him. "How about if we attack the two in the building, get them to send the alert, then pick off the rest with the Shell as they arrive?"

"Atrus doesn't know how many shots he can do before needing a recharge. And these things learn. I suspect any plan we do will only work once." Red lay on the cot, her hand rubbing her eyebrows.

"Well I don't know what else we can do. At least it is a chance. Do you have a better idea?"

"No," Red sat up, "all right Atrus, bring the Shell back and move it closer to those two and see what happens."

"Yes Mi … Red."

Red smiled as she watched the map. As the Shell moved in closer, the creatures moved back a bit, but not due to fear. "Atrus can you get a clear shot at one of them?"

"Yes I believe so." Atrus guided the Shell closer, and they looked out the window right in time to see a red energy bolt erupt from the Shell. A moment later one of the yellow dots vanished, and they heard an unearthly shriek. They knew it was a call to arms, and were not disappointed. The creatures that had since vanished from the map due to the Shell moving closer, reappeared and were moving fast.

"Okay that did it. Here they come!" Red said pointing. The yellow dots turning red as they expended more energy running. "Atrus! Take out the other one, *now*."

Atrus guided the Shell for another shot but before he could the creature leapt out the window. Atrus moved it to the right a second before impact. The creature fell several stories to land in the road head first, snapping its neck instantly.

"I don't think that one will trouble us anymore." James

pointed to the meat in the road. By now three more of the creatures arrived and howled over their dead comrade. Their eyes locked on Red and James. This howl was different. Their blood ran cold. "Atrus can you take out those as well?"

"Yes. One moment." Atrus said closing his eyes. The Shell hovered closer and red beams lanced out hitting all three in quick succession. They dropped to the ground with loud thuds.

"Nice shooting."

"Thank you Sir. But I regret to inform you that I have used 60% of the available power. I can't eliminate all of them."

"Great." James said gritting his teeth. By now five more of them arrived howling and flicking their tongues. One broke off from the pack and ran head long into the shield slamming with amazing force. It yelped in pain then passed out. "Well there is another one that probably won't bother us. Atrus take out the rest."

"Yes Sir." he said, a second later red beams lanced out hitting every creature. Each one fell in a heap.

"Very nice. And that is it for the Shell correct?" Red asked.

"Yes. Unfortunately the available power is too low. I can't use weapons again until the system recharges. Oh my, I have underestimated these creatures again."

"What?"

"Look at the map please, at the end of the road."

"I see a creature approaching very fast."

"Yes. However, did you notice the elevation?"

Red blinked. "It is flying?"

"Correct." But the words were barely spoken when a large creature with wings flew by. It had the same general lizard-lion look but larger than the others and it had leather wings that almost looked like some sort of pterodactyl. Except for the edges, which had feathers in various colors. They watched as it tried to grab the Shell, miss, then fly by and try again. It shrieked at every attempt. "It is after the Shell and the wind currents that creature is making it difficult to calculate the proper escape maneuver. I estimate it will catch it in the next few minutes."

"We can't let him catch it! I don't think I can create one from scratch!" James shouted. He turned towards Atrus. "You said you lacked the power to shoot, but it is still hovering. Can you use the hovering power to take one last shot?"

"Possibly. But the fall will likely damage it as much as the creature. And there are more creatures approaching."

"Then get low to the ground before you take the shot."

"Yes Sir." Atrus said as he guided the Shell lower, still keeping it out of the flying creatures reach.

"Okay *NOW!*" James said as the Shell hovered only two feet off of the ground and the creature dove for it. A red beam lanced out again but with the wind from the wings at the last second threw off the shot and it went wild blasting a rusted car instead. The Shell fell to the ground, its power exhausted. The creature landed and cautiously approached the Shell sniffing with its long tongue.

James had the gun in his hand quickly keying in a configuration. "Okay drop the front shield!"

"What?!" Red yelled. "Are you insane? They will kill you!"

"Atrus! Do it now! And raise it as soon as I am outside!"

"Yes Sir, shield down."

James dove out the door, rolled and came up his gun aimed directly at the creature who whirled at the sound and shrieked at him preparing to charge. James didn't even blink and pulled the trigger. A blue beam lanced out and hit the creature head-on causing it to explode outward in an ever expanding mushroom of dead flesh.

He heard sounds in the distance. More creatures coming, and by the sounds of it, all of them. Spinning around with his knee still in the dirt, he saw ten of them tightly grouped approaching at high speed. They would be on him in a few seconds. No time to shoot every one. But he was prepared for this.

James aimed his weapon at the lead creature and pulled the trigger.

A blue cone of raw power shot from the barrel leaving the strong smell of ozone in its wake. The energy slammed into the creatures vaporizing them causing the smell of burnt flesh as blood, muscle and bone expanded into raw power and then nothingness. When the dust settled, not one had survived.

James stood up and brushed himself off as Red ran out. She grabbed and held him tightly. "You are crazy you know that! Absolutely certifiable!"

He kissed her cheek and smiled. "Hey it worked didn't it?"

"Yes it did." She paused to grab his shoulders and shake in a rotating motion. "And if you *ever* do something like that again I am going to kill you. Got it?" she said smiling.

He smiled back. "Got it. And if I didn't know better, I would think you actually cared about me."

"Oh you think so?" She playfully punched him in the side then kissed him long and hard on the lips. "Whatever gave you that idea Mr. Moknkin?"

"I don't have a clue." His smile broadened as he gazed into her deep green eyes and squeezed her tightly.

Atrus flashed in front of them. "Excuse me during this important moment, but some creatures that attacked earlier may not be dead. I think it would be wise to either get back inside, or leave the area. Unless you can use that weapon again?"

"No I can't. Its charge is depleted now. So yes, it is time to go."

Red looked up to him. "How did you get the power level to change? You didn't have time to set it?"

"Ah, well I configured it to use the max setting on the second shot. I had hoped they would be running at me as a group. In general it is a sound idea, take out one, the others still get you. Unless you can eliminate the whole pack at once."

Red sighed. "You could have told me."

"Sorry there wasn't time." He said giving her a final squeeze and walking over to pick up the Shell laying in the dirt. "Doesn't look any worse for the wear. At least the creature didn't get a chance to play with it."

"Yes thankfully. And Sir?"

"Yes Atrus?"

"Next time you are going to do something 'creative' leave me with Miss Red?" Atrus said pointing to James' pocket.

"Atrus! What did I tell you about calling me that!"

"Oops, sorry Mi …Red it was a glitch in one of my algorithms."

"Atrus? Here is a tip, quit before you dig your grave any deeper," he said out the corner of his mouth.

Atrus blinked. "My grave?"

"Never mind. And by the way, why didn't Red run into the shield when she came out?"

"Oh I took the initiative and lowered the shield so she would not hit it. And after all, you had eliminated all the threats," he said with a grin.

Red walked over to James and put her arm around him. "Okay shall we go?"

"Do you know of a place we can jump?" James said giving Red another squeeze.

"Yes Atrus' map shows what I think is a parking lot, a couple of blocks north of us. I should be able to open a stable warp there."

"Wonderful, be back in a sec." James said as he handed her the Shell and ran inside. Red tried to ask where he was going, but he was already gone. A moment later he came reemerged with a black backpack.

"I needed something to carry the Shell in." He said as he stuffed it into the backpack. "Let's go."

A short time later, after wandering their way through the various building husks they found the parking lot. It wasn't empty, several rusted and blasted cars sat in their final resting places. But it was empty enough as most of them were around the outside leaving a large area in the middle open.

"I don't see how this area is going to help us leave?" Atrus said as he flashed into existence.

"You will." Red smiled as she got into a sprinters position. "Okay let's do this!" She bolted running counterclockwise. A moment later the air began to swirl.

"Oh my!" Atrus said. "She can run fast, such speeds shouldn't be possible."

"My friend you ain't see *nothing* yet." James said as Red continued to increase her speed. Dust and debris began to fly around in the storm. She increased again and a crack of lightning shot down striking the middle of the parking lot causing a rip in the very fabric of space and time. It was small, but it would quickly grow.

"What is that?" Atrus shouted his image constantly flickering due to the maelstrom.

"That is how we travel," James shouted.

"But this is not possible!"

James grinned. "Tell me about it!"

Then they heard a wail. A sound that shot a chill right through James. The one or more of the creatures had awakened. "Red! Hurry!" he shouted.

"I am trying! Almost ready!" She shouted back as they heard another sound, but much closer.

The warp continued to expand as Red increased her speed. "Go! NOW!" she shouted. James ran for the warp as one of the creatures appeared at the edge of the parking lot, but it was too late as James jumped into the warp with Red right behind him. The warp folded in on itself, vanishing right in front of its eyes.

— 16 —

A large bolt of blue lightning reigned down like fire from heaven striking the ground at the end of a long dirt clogged street. The streak quickly widened into the normal diamond shape flashing between blue and red. Arcs of raw power shot from the edges. A second later Red crashed out landing in the dirt with James landing on top of her a moment later.

"Ugh you need to lose weight," Red groaned.

"Hey! I put my hands out, hit the dirt first, and rolled off! I didn't land on you!"

"I know." Red said with a playful slap then rolled a bit closer, and slipped him a kiss. "Might be your new best friend on your back."

James laughed. "Nooo and you know it." James said as he kissed her back. "Okay when are we?"

Red sighed. "I don't know. Or where for that matter."

"But weren't you aiming for my time so we could set things right? I thought it was well within your range, and you were rested." James said climbing to his feet then helped Red up.

"Yesssss, but someone who shall remain nameless kept talking the whole time in the warp throwing off my concentration." Red said brushing the brown dust from her bodysuit.

Atrus flashed into existence before them. "Well you do have to admit it was a phenomenal experience. And you say we travel through that interdimensional conduit in space as well as time? Fascinating. The sensations were amazing."

"Atrus you are a computer. How can you feel?"

"An artificial intelligence Sir. Not just a computer. The electronic equipment I live in (what you like to call a computer) is only the outer part. Much like your brain is only the physical part of you."

"I stand corrected," James muttered.

Atrus' image bowed slightly. "Thank you Sir. But to answer your question, I can feel. Not quite the same as you of course, but I have various sensor inputs that are then fed into a system designed to mimic what a human would feel. I have control over the quantity of input or I can store it for later review. But in this case I couldn't help myself. Can we 'jump' again? I think that is what you called it?"

Red shook her head. "Not for a while. In your terms, my energy supplies have been drained and I need to recharge."

"I would have understood what you meant without the technical comparison."

Red smirked. "Oh? Are you sure?"

Atrus' eyes narrowed as he saw the humor that first evaded him. "Very funny Miss Red."

"Well what do you know? He can be taught," Red said as her smile broadened.

Atrus glared. "Very funny Miss Red."

"I thought so. And Atrus?"

"Yes?"

"Stop calling me Miss Red!"

"Sorry M . . . Red."

"Well I think we overshot our goal," James said with a loud sigh.

"Why do you say that?" Red asked.

James pointed. Straight up a very simple clothes line attached to a balcony with several items of clothing hanging from it. "Unless we landed in the middle of a Renaissance fair, I think that is a good indicator."

"Dang you are right. I would say 1400s judging by that." Red said looking up, then her nose wrinkled, and she fanned her hand quickly back and forth. "And the smell."

"Italy, between 1400 and 1430 I would say. Notice the headdress on the line, and the long flowing sleeves on the dress. They are obviously Italian in origin and fit in with the time frame I specified," Atrus said looking up.

"Well either way we are going to stand out like neon lights in a blackout," James said shaking his head.

"Well I definitely will," Red said gesturing at her bodysuit. "If you take your jacket off, I think you can pass."

"Pass? And do what?"

"Well get me some clothes I can wear. And perhaps yourself as well."

"With what? I don't have any money for Italy in the 1400s."

"They used the florin back then. It was a coin made of gold and weighed 54 grains or approximately 3.5 grams to use the modern standard of measurement," Atrus stated.

"Well thanks Mr. Encyclopedia. But I still don't have any!"

"You had better figure out something. I know I can't go walking around like this. I would attract too much attention."

Atrus raised his hand. "If I may suggest, I can use the Shell to grab the clothes hanging off the back of the building. Preliminary analysis indicates it should fit you M ... Red."

"How? It doesn't have arms to grab anything."

"Actually," James said sliding the backpack from his shoulder and removing one of the arms he replaced with a beam weapon earlier, "I grabbed them along with the bag right before we left."

Red carefully looked around the building in front of them. "I don't see anyone. Swap the arms and go for it."

James nodded. "Already done." He said raising the Shell sporting the new attachments. He then flipped the hidden power switch and closed the access panel. "Okay, Atrus you know what to do."

"Acknowledged. I have control." He said as the Shell hovered out of James' hand and rose up to the level of the clothes. It grabbed several items of clothing and hovered back down dumping them on Red as she looked around the corner.

"Hey! Watch it!" Red said as she looked at the items. The long blue dress, along with its various layers were heavy in her hands. She sighed as she began to put on them on. "I really hate fashion of this period."

"Sir I think Red could use some help." Atrus said after noticing Red struggling with the dress for several minutes.

"I wouldn't be if you got the right size. Preliminary scan my foot!" Red snorted still struggling. By now she had managed to get into the various layers but the back refused to close. James ran over and pulled several times until the buttons finally went into their holes.

"There you are. But don't take a deep breath." James said smiling looking up and down. The long dress pooled a bit around Red's feet. The elegant golden embroidery on the oversized sleeves matched buttons perfectly.

Red gave him a playful slap. "One word. Just one word and I will leave you next jump."

James smiled and slipped her a kiss. "No you wouldn't."

"Perhaps not, but I would be very tempted. Now where can we go? And I think you need something more than that if possible." Red said gesturing to James' black pants and jacket. "You may not be neon in a blackout, but the style does make you stand out a bit."

"Allow me." Atrus said as a long black robe dropped onto James' head the Shell had removed from a balcony a moment ago.

James pulled the garment off of his head. "Thanks Atrus."

"You are welcome Sir."

"Okay, I will go see if I can find out where we are. And Atrus?"

"Yes Sir?" Atrus said turning his holographic form towards him.

"Bring the Shell down. We can't take the chance of that being spotted."

"Yes Sir." Atrus said as the Shell slowly lowered into James hand. He opened the access panel, powered it off, then placed it in the backpack.

"Turn off your projection too." Red said looking back from the corner of the building. "The last thing we need is people here thinking we talk with ghosts."

"But I don't detect anyone in the vicinity and I can turn myself off the instant someone is in range."

"Atrus I know you like your image, but do as Red says. We can't take the risk."

Atrus hung his head. "Yes Sir." He said as his image flickered then vanished.

"All right, I will go see if I can find out when we are. If I remember right, a man in this time period will generate less interest asking odd questions than a woman." James said as he draped the simple long black robe over his shoulders and fastened the belt around his waist.

Red nodded. "You remember right."

"Thankfully Italian was covered some in my extended language course. Oh and Atrus?"

"Yes Sir?"

"Do not say or do anything unless I ask. Is that clear?"

"Yes Sir. I understand."

"Good." James leaned forward to slip Red a kiss. "Be back in a few minutes. You stay here."

Red chuckled. "Don't worry I don't plan ongoing anywhere like this unless I have to. I feel like I am wearing ten layers. No wonder women at this time fainted a lot."

"Yeah. I feel for you."

"No you don't," she playfully slapped him on the backside, "get going."

"I am. I am." James said as he walked down towards what appeared to be the main road. Reaching the front of the building proved what he feared. The sanitary conditions were deplorable as mentioned in the history books. The late afternoon sun glared as it peeked around the buildings.

James noticed a man slowly walking across the street some distance from him. James walked quickly and tapped the man on the shoulder as he was looking over the various buildings. "Mi scusi." James said in his best Italian, hoping it was close enough to not make the man suspicious.

"Si?" The man said turning towards James.

"What is the date today?"

"Why it is February 9th."

"And the year?"

The man looked at James up and down. "Why any fool knows it is 1428."

"Please forgive me, I am a stranger here and I wanted to make sure that more time didn't pass during my travel than I thought."

"Of course." The man said nodding and continued on his way.

By the time James got back to Red, the sun's rays had greatly weakened, and he found her huddled in the brace of the brick building.

"About time you got back. After the sun set, a breeze kicked up, and it is a bit cold. It must be winter, Italy is usually warmer than this."

"Yes you are right it is winter, 1428 to be exact. But at least it is not farther north or we really would be freezing. It is not that cold."

"Speak for yourself. We need a place for the night. Atrus?"

Atrus flashed before them. "Yes Red?"

"Is there anyplace nearby we might be able to use for the night?"

"Yes as a matter of fact, there is a near empty building with small rooms. It is at the end of this street. A storage facility of some sort I suspect."

"Thank you. And what did we say about your hologram?"

"Sorry Red, I will do better next time." Atrus said as his image nodded then faded.

James took Red's hand, and they walked between the two buildings to the main street. In the distance they could make out a building at the end and walked towards it. Thankfully, the increasingly dark street was deserted, and no one saw them approach. Looking around Red popped open the lock, and they slipped inside.

Inside a thin layer of flour dust covered everything. "Well this is a storage building all right, storage for a baker," Red said with a smirk.

"Well it should be okay for us tonight, I doubt he will be baking this time of day," James said looking around. "I see the smaller rooms towards the back I think." He pointed to the far wall.

Red nodded. "Let's get set up for the night. It is getting really cold around here." She said with a slight shiver.

James felt the shiver and wrapped his arm around her. In the back they found one of the rooms empty. "Well this isn't the Taj Mahal, but it will do."

Red laughed. "I have slept in worse than this before. And it is better than that cave we were in," she said poking him in the ribs.

"Oh I know." He said smiling, but when he felt her shiver again, he faced her and looked into her eyes. "Are you okay? It is not that cold."

"Yes it is, but you are too stubborn to admit it. Don't worry about me, I am fine."

"Okay but I can't have you sleep on the floor shivering like that. Oh, I have an idea." James said as he ran out of the room. He returned a couple of minutes later dragging several large flour sacks. "Here, these should help." He said while placing them in a makeshift bed. Red lay down and James covered her with the long cloak. "Now you get some rest." He said snuggling up to her holding tight.

"I will be fine." She said slipping him a kiss then quickly fell asleep.

Morning couldn't have come quick enough for James. Although he didn't want to admit it, it was rather cold, but not as cold as Red seemed to be. He tossed and turned restlessly and finally gave up resigning himself to watch over

Red. She slept soundly, never stirring once. By the time she did stir, sunlight was streaming into the windows.

"Ah, you are awake. How are you feeling?" James said as he turned his gaze from the door.

"Still tired but okay otherwise." She said stretching as she got to her feet. "Remind me to thank the hotel staff. Think we should clean up or let the maid do it?" she said gesturing around the room.

James chuckled. "Well we could, but probably best not to let him know someone slept on his flour."

"Yes probably not. *Ouch*!" Red said rubbing her leg.

"Red? What is wrong?"

"I don't know. I am getting odd muscle cramps. And wow it is warm in here all of a sudden." She stiffened, her eyes rolled back, and she went crashing down face first. James jumped forward, caught her, then carefully lowered her to the ground. He ran his finger tips across her forehead and his eyes widened, she was never this warm before.

"Atrus! Something is wrong with Red."

Atrus flashed into existence in front of him. "Please take me out of your pocket and hold vertically in front of your chest."

"What for?"

"Please do as I ask."

"All right." James said as he pulled Atrus from his pocket and held him out as instructed. A moment later a beam of horizontal light lanced out and touched Red's forehead. Then slowly moved down to her toes, back up to her head, repeated, then retracted.

"Scan complete. Oh no."

"What? What is wrong with her?"

"This can't be."

"What?"

“But I did the scan twice.”

“Atrus! Talk to me!”

“I am sorry Sir, but she has been infected with *Yersinia pestis.*”

“What! What is that?”

“Bubonic plague.”

“Plague! How long does she have?”

“Well we need to cure her within two days or the damage will be too extensive.”

“How? I didn’t bring any plague cures with me!”

“Sir, I have taken the liberty of scanning the history for this particular period and I may have a solution.”

“Which is?”

“Have you heard of Matteuccia di Francesco?”

“No I don’t think so. Who is she?”

“She was burned at the stake on March 20th 1428 after being branded a witch. Her herbalistic cures were labeled as witchcraft.”

“And how does witchcraft help us?”

“Sir as I said, her work was labeled as witchcraft. She wasn’t actually doing it. Some of them were total fantasy. Others were remarkably advanced.”

“And you know this how?”

“From what you call the *Voynich Manuscript.*”

“Wait! I have heard of that. Isn’t it in a code of some sort? No one has been able to read that for hundreds of years. Even the best code breakers couldn’t make any sense of it.”

“Well as you know I had time on my hands, and encryption always fascinated me. I managed to break the code. I admit it was complex, and some pages were missing which complicated the situation,” Atrus said.

“You actually cracked it? And how does it help us now?”

"Much of the data is related to botany and herbalistic cures. Of course most of it has no basis in fact as I said, but there is one part about the black death that might help us."

"You mean it had the cure to the bubonic plague? Well why didn't you say so in the first place! Tell me how to make it!"

"I can't."

"Why not?"

"While I was able to decode and understand the manuscript, there are pages missing. One page in particular is referenced as having the black death cure, and it is one of the missing pages."

"Can't we make one from my time?"

"With the equipment available now? Sadly it is not possible. We could eventually build something to distill and refine the raw elements we will need to create a vaccine. But Miss Red does not have that much time."

"Then what can we do?"

"Well you recall the gentleman earlier mentioning it was 1428?"

"Yes, February 9th if I remember right."

"Well at this point in time, she has been arrested on suspicion of witchcraft and is in jail."

"So? You are not saying we should go try to talk to her? They would burn us along with her!"

"No, nothing like that. If I can scan the original manuscript, we should be able to make the cure that Miss Red needs."

"And you are sure she has it? I thought they were never sure who wrote the *Voynich Manuscript*."

"Thankfully more information was found out about it after your time. But yes I am certain she created it. She was a very intelligent woman dedicated to the healing of others."

"Then why was she burned at the stake?"

"I assume she realized that her herbalistic concoctions would brand her a witch. Therefore, she encoded them into the manuscript. Not realizing that the news of the people she had helped would condemn her. From what I have been able to ascertain on this time period, if anyone were even remotely accused, they were always found to be a witch. Apparently, through torture. And in fact Matteuccia confessed to transforming into an insect the size of a fly after using a potion of her own making. However, by then I suspect she was willing to tell them anything, if they would stop. Also, her main accuser Bernardino of Siena had often given that exact phrase as an example of what witches could do. Further indicating torture was used to acquire the confession."

"Are saying that we need to break into her house, find the book, create what we need, and sneak back out before anyone spots us?"

"Yes. Very simple."

"Sure. Simple. And are you sure you are intelligent?" James snorted.

"Yes I am quite certain that my neural nets are–"

James raised his hand. "Never mind. Let's see if we can find her house."

After many strange looks from various people when he asked about Matteuccia, James finally found her small cottage on the outskirts of town. Finding the door unlocked, he let himself in. The strong fragrant smells of various herbs stuck him as he entered. Taking a deep breath, he let his nose guide his feet. Near the back, in a side room, he found her lab. In the corner lay a desk with ornate carved wooden panels on the side. Books and papers were strewn all over it. Glass bottles containing all sorts of odd items were sitting on large wooden shelves. In the center of the room, a flat wooden work table with a pedestal, mortar, and several jars that appeared to be used for mixing.

"Atrus!"

Atrus' hologram appeared in front of him. "Yes?"

"What am I looking for?"

"Well the manuscript preferably. Do you happen to see it on the desk?"

"No." James as he shuffled through the various books and papers on the desk. "And it looks like someone else been here. Either that or she was in the middle of something when she was arrested."

Atrus nodded. "Yes I agree."

"I hoped that it was hidden under something else, but I don't see any sign of it." James let out a long sigh. "I don't know what to do."

"Sir, if I may offer a suggestion. Hold me out in front so that I may do an intensive scan."

"All right." James said nodding as he held Atrus in front of his chest. A green horizontal beam shot out as before quickly going from the top of the desk to the bottom. It repeated this several times before retracting.

"Fascinating."

James blinked. "What? What did you find?"

"Sir, I suggest you pull the first drawer out one inch, the second two inches, and the third drawer out all the way."

"What will that do?"

Atrus smiled. "Humor me."

James reached down to the vertical rows of drawers on the one side, and pulled the first one out, then the second, and finally the third although it pulled much harder than the other two. When it was fully extended, he heard a soft click. "Did you hear that?"

"Yes. Please check the carved wooden panel on the side. I think you will find it will swing open."

Sure enough, as soon as James touched the panel it creaked open revealing a book in a hidden compartment. "Well well well look what we have here. This woman is smarter than I gave her credit for." He said removing the book from its hiding place. "And how did you know?"

"If you recall, I said that she was far advanced for her time. When I scanned the desk, I found the book in the recess. Then it was a simple matter of locating the unlocking mechanism. Now if you will turn to page 32, I think that page holds the answers we seek."

"32? Okay." James said flipping through the various brightly colored pages silently counting. "Ah, here it is. It looks like several plants with a bunch of gibberish. Are you sure you can read this?"

"Quite certain. It would appear that she not only encoded the words, but also the ingredients."

"What does that mean?"

"Well she only says use a certain amount of the contents of a numbered jar. But not what the actual jar actually contains."

"She was really cautious. I am surprised she was branded a witch without any evidence." James said shaking his head before sitting in the hard chair next to the desk.

"Yes she was. But you have to realize that people of this time didn't need much substantiation. All they need was suspicion. Then evidence was changed or created to match. From what I can determine, this was mostly done out of fear. Fear of the unknown."

"You are probably right. Are you sure we can create what we need?" James said as he gestured around the room.

"Yes. First take the third bottle on the right from the top shelf and grind it to a powder using the pedestal and mortar."

"Okay." James said as he stood and walked over to the shelves. Finding the bottle that Atrus had mentioned he popped the cork. The strong scent made his nose wrinkle. "Garlic."

"Garlic is known to kill many forms of pathogens," Atrus said nodding.

"And how much of this?"

"The instructions indicate two pedestals full."

"All right." James said as he put the garlic into the pedestal and ground it to a pulp. Juice oozed out of it and the strong smell made his eyes water. After a few moments he had enough and placed it into one of the empty jars on the table. "Okay what's next?"

"Eight pedestal measures of the liquid in the sixth bottle on the same shelf."

James popped the cork and sniffed. "Vinegar." He said measuring out the proper amount and pouring it into the jar.

"Also well-known for its healing properties. The rest appear to be solid herbs you will need to grind into a fine powder. Use jar eight, ten, and eleven."

"Okay got them." James said as he plucked the various bottles from the shelves. "And are you sure we shouldn't have carried Red here? It felt wrong to leave her."

"She will be fine. You activated the Shell before we left and I am monitoring her. Should it be necessary, I can stun whoever comes in."

"Yes, I know, but that didn't make leaving her any easier. Are you sure you can stun them from the bag without them actually seeing the Shell? I don't want them waking up shouting about flying demons breathing fire."

"Yes I am certain. They will never see anything of consequence."

"Good. Now how much of these do I use?"

"One mortar measure each. Then five measures of bottle thirteen, and two measures of the last bottle on the bottom shelf and that will be everything." Atrus pointed to each as he spoke.

"Well I will tell you one thing." James said as he continued to pound the various herbs into powder. "If nothing else this will certainly clear out her sinuses. It has mine and I have not taken any of it." He blinked through watery eyes.

A moment later he grabbed the last two bottles. "This one must be honey. But I have no idea what the other one is."

"Comfrey root Sir. Also known for its healing properties."

"Never heard of it, but let's hope it works." James said with a shrug as he finished measuring the last of the ingredients. "Now what do I do?"

"Mix it well and give to the patient is all it says."

"With what?" James said looking around. "I don't see anything I could use to mix it."

"Use the glass top at the end of the table and shake hard. I assume that is what she must have done."

"I will do that later. Let's get out of here, I don't want us to be seen."

"Not to worry Sir, there is no one in the area."

"Good, let's get this back to Red." James said as they left the lab and slipped out of the house. Back in town, he managed to meander his way past various early afternoon crowds along the streets and get back to Red without being noticed.

Inside, he found Red still asleep. "Red? Wake up. Please wake up."

She stirred. "What?" she said sleepily. "Can't I sleep a little longer? I really ache."

"Yes I know. We made something to help."

Her eyes shot open, and she sat up with a groan. "Made what?"

"This." James said as he removed a bottle from inside his cloak shook it a few times and handed it to her. All the walking with it in his pocket had done a decent job, but the last few shakes thoroughly mixed the concoction.

"And what am I to do with this?"

"Drink it."

"Are you sure?"

"Yes. Please, just do it."

"Okay okay." She said pulling off the glass top and took a sip. "Ugh this is disgusting!"

"Red you need to drink all of it. You have Bubonic plague. This will cure you."

"Bubonic plague?! How did you make this? Are you sure it will work?"

Atrus' hologram appeared in front of them. "Yes I am certain it will have the desired effect. I have analyzed the chemical compounds used and your infection is in its early stages. This should work in about twelve hours, given your increased metabolism."

Red held her nose and gulped down the rest of the foul liquid. "Ugh I don't know what is worse, the disease or the cure."

James blinked. "Bubonic plague? Are you kidding? You know–"

Red looked back at him smiling. "I was kidding. I am quite

familiar with the disease, and what it is capable of. What I don't understand is how I was infected."

"I think I may have found the answer to that. I anticipated your question and did several scans through the Shell while you were asleep and found an infected flea. Apparently it was left in the room by some form of rodent before we arrived."

"A infected flea? Then what is to prevent it from infecting me again? Or James for that matter."

"Not to worry, I shot it with the Shell and vaporized it." Atrus said pointing to the backpack with the top flap that was moved back enough to show the tip of a laser arm. "Thankfully it had jumped off of your clothes when you moved in your sleep."

James glared at Atrus. "And why didn't you tell me this before now?"

"I didn't see any reason to concern you, the situation was handled. And if you recall, you were very busy preparing the cure for M … Red."

"Yes. However, next time tell me. No matter how busy I am if it has anything to do with Red's safety. Am I clear?"

"Yes, I understand. I shall not do that again."

Red brought her knees to her chest and hugged them tightly. "Thank you both. I think I am starting to feel a little better. But very tired." She yawned then lay back down. "I need to sleep."

"Yes you sleep. We will watch over you." James said as he covered her with his cloak and tucked it around her. He smiled and slipped out of the room. The sun had long since set and the light was quickly waning inside the storehouse. James sat near the window and looked out. "Atrus?"

"Yes Sir?"

"Are you certain she will recover?"

"Yes I believe so. I can't be 100% certain of course, but what she drank should kill the infection. We will know in the morning."

James leaned against the edge of the window. "Well then I guess we should prepare for a long night."

"Sir, I can keep watch, you need to rest as well. If anything develops, you will be the first to know," Atrus said as the Shell hovered into view.

"For a moment I forgot about that. All right, I will try to get a little sleep." James said as he walked back to the other room and lay down next to Red. She stirred a little as he wrapped his arm around her and squeezed tenderly. A minute later he was fast asleep.

Red woke in the early morning and stretched as she sat up. James turned from the door where he was standing. "Oh good you are awake. Are you okay?" He said as he approached and sat down beside her.

"Yes, I think so. At least I feel much better. I don't have the aches I did last night. And it doesn't feel so cold in here."

James touched her forehead. "I don't think you have a fever." He pulled Atrus from his pocket. "Atrus scan her please."

"Yes of course. Red, please close your eyes. The light is rather intense." Red nodded closing her eyes. A moment later the scan was complete. "The infection is greatly reduced, and should be completely eradicated in the next couple of hours."

"Good. I am anxious to get out of here. I never did like this time period."

"Are you able to open a warp?" James asked.

"Yes I think so. We will give it a try this afternoon. And what was in that you gave me?"

"Well perhaps it is best you don't know," James smiled.

Red's eyes narrowed. "Will you at least tell me how you found it?"

James sat back against the wall. "Okay, okay, don't give me that look." James said waving his hands in front of him. "Do you know of the *Voynich manuscript*?"

"Yes. It is a very old book in an odd language. I always wondered who wrote it and why."

"I think we may have found out," James said smiling.

"Don't tell me, the cure was in that book?"

James nodded. "Yes. Atrus had decoded the book long before we met him."

Atrus' hologram resolved in front of them. "Yes and while I didn't know the formula, there were references to it on pages that had long since went missing."

"I see, and who wrote it?"

James smiled. "Hold on to your hat, Matteuccia di Francesco."

"Matteuccia? Wait a minute! Wasn't she burned at the stake for witchcraft?"

Atrus nodded. "The one and the same. But I was able to determine it was her advanced techniques in botany and healing that people didn't understand. Which brought about her predicament."

"Don't tell me you broke into a dead woman's house?"

"Of course not," James said, "she's not dead yet."

Red covered her eyes while shaking her head. "I don't think I want to hear anymore."

"Well there isn't much else to tell anyway," Atrus grinned.

James' eyes narrowed at the hologram in front of him. "Atrus?"

"Yes Sir?"

"Be quiet."

"Yes Sir," Atrus said as his hologram vanished.

Later that afternoon when the streets were empty of people, they slipped out of the storehouse and were walking quickly along the road leading out of town.

Red munched on a granola bar as they walked. "I am glad you grabbed a few of these before we jumped."

"I thought they might come in handy. Thankfully that food alcove knew how to make take out." James chuckled while crunching on one of his own.

"You said there was a clearing not far from here?"

"Yes. Atrus and I saw it when we were going to Matteuccia's. It is on the other side of this hill. Are you sure you are up to jumping? We can rest another day."

"No. I want out of this time." Red said stopping and turning her back towards James. "Now would you please get me out of this thing!"

"Oh sure." James said and quickly unfastened each button on the dress.

Red breathed a sigh of relief. "Thank you. Now why didn't you do that last night?"

"Because I thought you would be cold?" he said sheepishly.

"Good answer. I don't believe you. But a good answer."

"Red, I think that James is being–"

"Shut up. You are also a man and I don't believe you either in this case."

"But M . . . Red I am not–"

"I said be quiet and if you are wise, you will drop this."

Atrus raised an eyebrow still slightly perplexed at her comments but, decided not to press the issue further. "Consider it dropped."

The sun had set by the time they reached the clearing. It was as James remembered: large enough for Red to run and the hill behind should keep anyone from town spotting them. Red dropped the rest of the heavy clothes along the road. "I am certainly not going to miss those," she said stretching. "Are you both ready?"

"Ready when you are," James said.

Red lowered herself into a sprinting position. "Okay let's do this!" And she bolted running clockwise faster and faster. After a few moments an energy bolt shot down in the middle opening the warp. Red continued to increase her speed with leaves, dust and dirt swirling around in her wake.

"Truly fascinating," Atrus said.

"Atrus?"

"Yes Sir?"

"Make sure you are quiet from now on. I don't want you to throw off Red again? Is that understood.?"

"Acknowledged. Although I wouldn't have even if you didn't tell me. I do learn, remember?"

"I just thought it was wise to mention it."

"If you two are finished bickering hurry up and …*jump* …*NOW!*"

"Oops sorry!" James shouted as he jumped into the warp with Red right behind him.

As the warp closed a man in the distance wearing a stained bakers apron stood with his eyes wide. After following what he thought must have been two thieves leaving his storehouse, he was simply relieved they were gone. He considered asking around to see if anyone else had seen them, then thought better of it. They weren't carrying anything, so they couldn't have been thieves. And there was no way he was going to tell anyone what he saw. "I would end up in the cell next to Matteuccia," he muttered to himself as he headed back to town.

"What do you mean they disappeared??" Director Ridblam said his face flush with anger as he stood from behind his desk and placed both palms on it. "No one leaves this building without leaving some kind of trail!"

Agent Kirby stiffened as he stood in the doorway. "We don't know director. She is not in the building, we have checked everywhere." He took a deep breath before continuing in a quieter tone. "We also can't find Agent Moknkin either."

"You mean one of our own agents helped a terrorist assassin escape?" Ridblam shouted as he leaned closer to Kirby.

Kirby stiffened further. "Well if he did, he didn't leave a trail either. If he used his access codes to leave, there would be logs. But all we have is when he enters and leaves Professor Keleeigan's lab. Then he disappears. He never left that floor as far as we can tell."

"Moknkin was last seen at Keleeigan's? Then get him in here NOW! And I want those two agents that were posted to guard the woman in front of me yesterday. Is that clear?"

"Crystal clear Sir." Agent Kirby said as he turned on his heel and left.

An hour later Agent Kirby pushed Keleeigan rather strongly into the chair opposite Director Ridblam and stood in the doorway. Keleeigan grunted while looking Ridblam up and down trying to size the man up. "I hope this is important, I am in a very delicate phase of repairing–"

Ridblam raised his hand. "I assure you it is. Now when was the last time you saw Agent Moknkin?"

"James?" Keleeigan said sitting back in the chair. "Is that what all this is about?"

"Yes. And I will repeat, when was the last time you saw him?" Ridblam said his hands folded on top of a stack of papers marked classified.

"Earlier today. He picked up the new prototype energy pistol I have been working on for testing. We talked for a few minutes, then he left," Keleeigan said with a shrug.

Ridblam's eyes narrowed. "He has the weapon? Do you think he could be a traitor?"

"James!?" Keleeigan laughed as he stroked his white hair. "You must be joking."

"I can assure you I am not," Keleeigan said his face stern.

The professor sat forward in his chair. "Well let me put whatever fears you have to rest. I have not met a more dedicated and loyal person in all of my life. It is why I trusted him with my most powerful project to date. I have known him since he was a boy, all he ever wanted to do was join the bureau and serve his country. This is not a man that betrays the one thing he has held dear for all of his life."

"Perhaps."

Keleeigan's eyes narrowed. "Perhaps nothing. Now let me ask you, *what* is going on?"

"I am afraid that is classified at the moment."

Keleeigan snorted. "I think you will find my clearance level goes beyond yours. Don't toy with me director. I have a lot of contacts, and you could easily find yourself classified as a security risk in the blink of an eye." He leaned further in his chair meeting Ridblam's gaze. "So I will ask again, what is this all about?"

"All right, I suppose you are entitled to know considering your prototype was stolen."

Keleeigan blinked. "Stolen? I never said it was stolen. I told you James took it for testing. He should be returning it right after he completes those tests."

"Well in that, we have a problem. You see, we can't locate Agent Moknkin. The last time his clearances were used was when he visited your lab. There is no indication he ever left the floor, yet he is missing along with a woman we believe is a terrorist trying to kill the president."

Keleeigan sat back in his chair. "There is no chance that James would ever be a party to such a situation," he said with a dismissive wave of his hand. "Who is this supposed terrorist?"

Ridblam stood and walked over to the window gazing out. The late afternoon sun shone brightly. "We don't know. Her fingerprints do not coincide with any known terrorist or organization. She was being held down the hall from the south entrance to your lab." Ridblam's voice tone lowered almost to a whisper as he turned towards Keleeigan. "When we lost her."

"Lost her? What do you mean lost her? How could you lose someone on my floor? It is the most secure in the whole building!"

"I am well aware of that Professor. Still, it is what happened. Did you notice anything strange earlier today?"

"Apart from some sort of power surge that blew out one

third of my computer systems that I think was from a lightning strike. No."

"What? Why didn't you tell me about this beforehand?"

"Because I have been busy trying to salvage what is left! I would have told you once everything has been stabilized. At this point it is more important to save what I can."

Ridblam cocked an eyebrow. "I assume you have backups?"

"Of course I do! But this surge was massive and somehow traveled down the direct line to the data storage facility I use and fried the archives there. I have never seen anything like it. I wish I could have studied it in more detail."

Ridblam again looked out the window and to the traffic below. "I see. Considering that Moknkin is missing, I suggest you begin work on making another prototype of that weapon as soon as possible. How long will it take?"

"Years, perhaps never, at least until James returns."

"What?! Why?!" Ridblam shouted as he spun on his heel to face Keleeigan.

Keleeigan shook his head. "I am sorry. That is one of the areas of the database that was totally fried."

"So you are telling me that he not only made off with the prototype but it can never be recreated? And how can you still think he is not involved?"

"Yes I am sure he is not. It is an odd coincidence, nothing more. And I didn't say it could never be recreated, only that it will take a lot of time unless we find James. You see there is a backup copy of the entire plans stored inside the prototype's memory."

Ridblam paused for a moment as the enormity of that sunk in. "You put the plans inside one of the most powerful weapons that has ever been developed allowing them to walk out of here at any point? Are you insane?"

"Hardly. I was being cautious. And giving the situation now with my database, I think I made a good one. James will return, have no fear."

"I do have fears. Fears you should not have the clearances to be in this building and I am going to get them revoked."

"Try it," Keleeigan smirked and folded his arms, "you have no chance and you know it."

"Don't tempt me Professor," Ridblam said sitting back down in his chair. "Now I suggest you get back down to your lab and see what else you can recover."

"About time. It is what I was doing before I was so rudely interrupted." He said standing and turned to leave then paused and turned back. "Oh you never said how the woman disappeared. The supposed terrorist? I assume you have talked with the agents that were guarding her."

"I have. And I think they were drinking on the job, using some sort of hallucinogenic substance, or something was used on them without their knowledge. I have both men confined and we are running tests."

"Why? What happened?"

Ridblam sat back in his chair and began to turn it back and forth. "The men started to hear a howl, almost as if a hurricane was in the integration room. Then the sound of thunder a second later. They managed to open the door with difficulty, then it flew off its hinges. In the middle of the room was some sort of strange phenomenon. One said it looked like an angry eye. The other talked about a rip in the middle of the room with arcs of lightning emanating from the edges. Either way they both mention an intense wind that almost pulled them inside. A moment later it was gone, and they were on the floor."

The Keleeigan eyebrows went up. "Curious. Is there any proof of what they described?"

"Some yes. The table was missing. Both the chairs and door showed considerable damage. We originally thought that some sort of explosion that backfired and killed her when she was trying to escape. But after Agent Moknkin turned up missing, we started to think she did escape with Moknkin's help. And this was all a cover up."

Keleeigan shook his head. "I told you it is not possible that James would help a terrorist. But the tale is fascinating. Where there any video to corroborate what they said?"

"No," Ridblam said flatly, "all we have is her placing chairs on the middle of the table and start running around it. A second later the camera fails."

"What about the one in the hallway?"

"That one failed as well, the hardware was fried similar to the other, at the exact same moment in fact."

"And you think James did all of this?"

"I think it is possible, yes."

"Then you are a bigger fool than I thought. There is no way James could have damaged both cameras and my lab simultaneously with such power. Something very unusual happened today, of that I am certain. And far beyond what you are thinking." Keleeigan said and quickly walked out before the director could say anything more.

The air began to swirl blowing the moonlit grass. A few leaves were picked up and joined in as the wind increased. A moment later lightning struck the ground, and a rip opened in its wake. It grew in size as the storm intensified. Suddenly the rip grew, fluctuated, and James crashed out on his back with Red landing right on top of him. The jagged gash slammed shut with a loud crash a microsecond later.

"Oh I love it when you are on top," he said giving her a peck on the check.

"Be quiet you," she said with a playful slap then kissed him back. "We don't know if there is anyone around," she said getting to her feet.

James quickly looked around then jumped to his feet as well. "I think we can rule out a large crowd of people seeing us land," he said gesturing to the wide expanse. "There is no one around," his eyebrows rose as he spun around. "This looks like some kind of park."

Atrus flashed into existence in front of them. "There is no one in my scanning range."

"Thank you Atrus," James said.

"You are welcome Sir." Atrus said as he bowed slightly before his image winked out.

Red rolled her eyes. "He sticks up for you a bit too much." She took a deep breath as she brushed herself off. "Hopefully this is Washington D.C. shortly after we left. If not then we will have to try again."

"Hey, I recognize those fountains," James said pointing to the water feature lit by moonlight in the distance. "This is Senate Park. Upper section I think." He turned around and walked past a line of trees. In the distance, the well-lit Capitol Dome stood out. "Yes we are definitely in D.C."

Red smiled seeing the dome. "Good for once we hit where I aimed. Atrus?"

Atrus appeared before her. "Yes Red?"

"Can you access the local time from the USA atomic clock? They broadcast on 60khz."

"Yes I can and already have assumed your request. You have arrived eight hours after you left this time-line. Providing the information you gave me previously is accurate."

"Oh it is Atrus, trust me."

Atrus nodded slightly in her direction. "Oh I do Miss Red, always," he said before his image winked out.

Red growled. "I wish he would stop calling me that." She looked around again trying to get her bearings. "Now let's grab my backpack. It's not far."

"Now? Shouldn't we, oh I don't know, try to save the president?"

"Listen if I had it, we wouldn't have taken near so long getting back here."

"Why?"

Red sighed. "Look, I only told you some of what was in it. There is one item that I really don't want to lose."

"Which is?"

"A headband."

"You want to get a headband that badly? We can get you one anywhere," James laughed.

"It is no ordinary headband. In the middle of the forehead area contains a crystal. The crystal apparently was from some sort of meteorite. Or so I was told."

"What is so special about it?"

"It is harder than diamond and helps me focus my thoughts while in the warp. And don't ask me how it works, as I don't know. Remember when I had to go back and stop the explosives I set previously from destroying the bridge?"

"Yes."

"Well I managed to get to that point in one jump. I couldn't have done that without the crystal."

"Wow. It really enhances your accuracy that much?"

Red nodded. "Yes, it would have likely taken many tries and any failure in that case could have damaged the timeline further. And if I had it now, we could have been back here long ago. I can't imagine getting another one. While I can jump without it. The difference feels like night and day."

"Okay let's go get it."

Red smiled. "We? Don't you think you had better report in or whatever you do?"

James nodded. "Of course. But that can wait a bit. Besides, I am not exactly sure how I should contact them. Using the normal methods would be problematic. I'm certain they are working on the assumption I willingly left with you, a likely assassin and possible terrorist. Not to mention, you might need help to get the pack."

"It should be this way, at the edge of the park, in a storm drain."

"You hid it in a storm drain?"

"Yes, if you recall I didn't expect to be gone long. Originally I thought my information would have convinced them of the truth. Instead, they branded me as a terrorist and held me against my will." Red shook her head. "I won't trust them again."

"Well you must admit it is an unusual situation. And we are trained to not trust something given that easily as it will likely be a ploy." James said as they walked across the park towards the road he knew was Delaware Avenue.

"Yes I know. But still, I was trying to save the future. And all I got for it was a lot of accusations and grief."

James wrapped his arm around her and squeezed. "Well you did get more than that." He smiled.

She squeezed back and gave him a peck on the cheek. "Perhaps."

James' eyes narrowed. "What do you mean, perhaps?!"

"Shhh," she said putting a finger to his lips. "Anyone ever tell you're cute when you're mad?" She kissed him again on the cheek before he could respond. "It is over here." She pointed to a rusted grate along the side of the road. But when she tried to lift the metal grid, it refused to budge.

"I don't understand it. It was so easy before."

"I think I see the problem. There is a lock hanging down on the other side. I would guess men were working here and left the grate unlocked. But then remembered and locked it after."

Red squinted in the dim light trying to look through the grate. "I don't see my pack, I think they must have got it. How will I ever find it now?" Red sat down on the curb, her head in her hands.

"I wouldn't jump to conclusions yet."

Atrus' hologram appeared before them. "Nor would I. I have scanned this underground structure, and I have located your backpack directly below us. If I may suggest, James' gun could simply vaporize the grate."

James shook his head. "I can't do that. There would be too many questions as to how it happened. Not to mention cars or other people could fall in. However, on a low setting I might be able to cut the lock off." James said pulling out the weapon and flipping open the control panel and tapped in several commands. "Okay let's see what this does."

"Wait!" Red said holding out her hand. "Are you sure about this?"

"No, but I can see the lock, and I know you can't pick it since it is out of your reach. This should work. Don't worry this setting won't vaporize the grate."

"You hope," Red said getting up and taking several steps in the opposite direction.

"Gee thanks for the vote of confidence." He pulled the trigger. A small red beam shot from the barrel, through one of the holes in the grate, and stuck the lock vaporizing it instantly.

Red shoved him. "You vaporized it! What would have happened if you missed?"

James grinned. "But I didn't, did I?" He grabbed the grate and pulled it up without too much effort. His other hand dove in, plucked Red's pack from its hiding place, and handed it over. "I believe this is yours."

She took it gingerly. "Yes that looks like it." She placed her thumb on a zipper, and after an almost inaudible beep the bag unzipped with ease. Inside all was as she left it. "It is all here, the headband, spare suit, and even the energy bars."

"Energy bars? We do have them you know."

"Not these you don't. They are a special type of bar that contain far more nutrients and digestible energy than anything available in your time. I like to keep a few on hand in case I need them. Generally, I only use them during emergencies as they aren't that easy to replace."

"I see," James said lowering the grate back down.

"Well now that we have my pack, how shall we go about saving your president."

"My president?"

"Well remember I am not from this time-line. At least I don't think so." Red shrugged. "And last time I tried, it didn't work out very well. So how about you tell me how we should go about it?"

"Okay, first off you mentioned evidence that you showed them. What exactly was it?"

"I suggest both of you move to another location. There is a vehicle approaching," Atrus said as his hologram winked out.

"Good idea," Red said as they walked away from the street. "Well I had a detailed history of where exactly the president was for the next three days."

"You mentioned that. And most of it is not top secret. I'm not sure why they held you for knowing where he was for the next three days."

"I also had a video of him dying."

James' eyes went wide. "You had a video of him dying? No wonder they freaked out. I assume they thought it was a fake?"

"Yes they did, but apparently it worried them enough to keep me and try to find out more than what I was telling them."

"How does he die?"

"In a hospital from ricin poisoning."

"Ricin! How?"

"It took some doing but eventually I found another video during a phone call to Russia he swats at something. Almost like a mosquito had bitten him. At first, I thought that was when it happened. However, this video doesn't show anyone in the room."

"You're sure there isn't anyone else in the room at the time?"

"Yes, although one door opens seemingly on its own. But the video cameras inside the Oval Office and outside do not show anything unusual. This I could never explain, which is why I never told anyone else."

"Do you have the videos now?"

"Yes I have the originals, they are on a chip I have in my pack." She said unzipping and handing over a tiny square smaller than a fingernail. "Although I don't know what can read it in this time."

James smiled. "Oh I think I do. Atrus?"

"Yes Sir?" he said but his hologram didn't appear.

"What no hologram?"

"I have detected someone in the distance and you always told me to be discreet when using it."

"Very true. Thank you. Now, can you read this device and extract the video?"

Atrus' image flickered before them. "Yes if I downgrade myself." He said with a smirk then raised a hand. "Don't worry the person has left the area. And if you hold the chip in direct contact with me, I will be able to read it."

James removed Atrus from his pocket and placed the chip on top of the device. "Okay how about now?"

"Yes. Data recovered. Hmm very unusual."

Red blinked. "What is?"

"The video that you spoke of with the president in the Oval Office. I think I may have found something. I can display it if you like."

James nodded. "Yes please do."

A second later a two-dimensional image appeared in the air. The president was clearly talking on the phone. A moment later the door opens. He stops to look out from his desk, but not seeing anyone, continues with the call. A few seconds later he swats at something on his neck but appears to continue unaffected.

"I don't see anything odd other than the door opening."

"Nor do I. It is the same old vid I have seen. I think the ricin was delivered at that point, but how is the question. And being I can't prove anything, I didn't show this to anyone else," Red said with a shrug.

"Ah but I do see something. It is on a different wavelength. Let me show you." Atrus said and a moment later the video replayed but this time a red figure with the rough shape of a man walks in after the door is opened. The shape aims towards the president's neck. Then walks out a few seconds later.

"Whoa! What was that?" Red said blinking.

"I am not certain due to quality of this video, but from what I can ascertain the assassin wore a type of clothing or device that made him invisible. But he couldn't totally hide his heat signature. I had to enhance it over ten thousand times for you to see it," Atrus said.

Red looked at Atrus. "He? How are you sure it is man?"

"The highest points of thermal imagery indicate a reproductive system in the groin area rather than abdominal."

"Well that would be a good indicator," James chuckled.

Red sat on the nearest bench. "What is our next step? You know these people better than I."

James sat down beside her as Atrus walked his hologram over as well. "I was thinking of contacting Keleeigan, but any route I use would likely draw an immediate alert. I suppose we should try to find a payphone. I think there is one a bit north of here." He leaned forward, his arms on his knees and hands folded. "But I will have to be careful what I say, and we will have to move fast as I'm sure they will put a trace on the call."

"Sir, if I my make a suggestion, I can access the communications grid for you."

James sat up. "You can?"

"Oh yes, I have been analyzing the system ever since we arrived. It is very noisy you know, and quite primitive. Security was never really implemented. I am surprised the system works at all," Atrus said shaking his head. "Who do you wish me to contact?"

"Look up Moris Keleeigan at the FBI. I forget his private number, but hopefully the public one will work well enough for us. Too bad we can't make a private call or block their trace."

Atrus smiled. "Sir, I can do that as well, if you do not wish them to know our location, they will not. Encrypting the call is also not a problem either."

James blinked. "How? Wouldn't he need decryption gear on his end as well?"

Atrus' smile broadened. "With your primitive method of encryption yes. However, I have located his phone, and it does have enough memory. I can reprogram it to decrypt the call, then self-terminate after. No trace will be left."

"All right," James grinned, "go for it." He turned towards Red, his smile growing wider. "And you didn't want to bring him along."

Red raised her hands. "Okay okay I stand corrected."

"Link created Sir. Would you like video as well or audio only?"

"No need to frighten him, just audio."

"Done. Call has been received, relaying audio."

"Hello?" Keleeigan's strong voice came through clearly.

"Hi Doc!"

"James! You shouldn't have called. Do you realize that

the bureau has red flagged you? They will be on you in a minute."

"Don't worry I have that taken care of. We can talk."

"How can–"

"Never mind. Listen, first off I assume that everyone thinks I am helping terrorists?"

"Yes. Ridblam had me in his office earlier today. I can't say that was an enjoyable experience. He even tried to threaten me! Me! I have more clearance than most of the people in this building!"

"I am sorry, I certainly never wanted to cause you problems."

"Don't worry about it my boy. I can have him thrown out on the curb if I wanted to. He can't touch me and he knows it. Or he would find out if he tried. I almost want him to make the attempt," Keleeigan said chuckling. "Now what is going on?"

"Well how much do you know? Or perhaps I should ask, what did Ridblam say?"

"He said you were likely helping a terrorist as they had one in holding a few doors down from my lab when she escaped. Since your codes were last used on my door and nowhere else, they assumed you were involved. I told him he was crazy, but that didn't go far."

"Anything else?"

"Well apparently the guards told a fantastic tale about some sort of phenomenon with a strange storm. Ridblam thinks they were drugged. But I do know that an unusual power surge fried a great portion of my database. Oh by the way, how does the prototype work outside of the lab? I assume you still have it with you?"

"Yes I have it. And it works great. Now I need to tell

you, what the guards said was true. There was a strange phenomenon at that time, and I was drawn into it by accident. That is where I have been."

Keleeigan paused for a moment. "Are you talking teleportation? I had a general theory of it but we are years from any–"

"No not teleportation. I can't go into details right now, and while no one can listen in on our conversation, I am sure that our long talk that can't be heard has raised a few eyebrows. Listen, the so called terrorist was actually someone that had evidence of a plot to kill the president to take place in three days time. Because of her detailed knowledge of the presidents movements, she was labeled a terrorist or at least an unwitting party."

"I see," Keleeigan paused to take a deep breath, "and what do you need from me?"

"Can we meet somewhere? It would best if I show you rather than tell you."

"Most of my movements around here are likely tracked. Let's see. Oh I know. Do you remember that diner where we used to have lunch at because your father said they made the best hot dogs?"

James laughed. "Oh yes. Are they still around? I haven't looked in years."

"They are. Shall we meet in say one hour?"

"Agreed." James said as the connection closed then turned towards Red. "I hope we can beat Ridblam there, Doc's lab is well monitored by audio and video pickups. They probably know everything."

Atrus shook his head. "No they won't. I took the liberty of disabling the system by flooding them with white noise during your conversation. If anyone was watching, or reviews the recordings they will only assume a hardware failure occurred."

"Thank you Atrus."

Atrus bowed slightly. "You are welcome Sir. And if I may make another suggestion?"

Red folded her arms and glared at Atrus. "What now?"

"That I procure you a vehicle? We need to travel some distance in two hours, and this is unlikely without a vehicle."

"And how are you going to do that?"

Atrus smiled. "The network I have accessed also has databases of vehicles for hire. I can get one for you and have it delivered."

"That is well and good, but my credit cards are likely being watched."

"Such a primitive form of monetary transactions. And so few safeguards in place. I can't imagine how your system continues to function at all." Atrus paused for a moment as if lost in concentration. "There. A vehicle will arrive in a few moments and as far as they are concerned, have been paid in advance."

"Thank you Atrus."

"You are welcome Sir." He said bowing slightly as his image winked out.

"And you wanted to leave it him behind." James nudged Red with his elbow.

"Oh shush." She grumbled her folded arms going tighter. "You are never going to let that go are you?"

He slipped her a kiss. "Perhaps, someday, but not now." He kissed her again. "Anyone ever tell you, you are sexy when you pout?"

"Oh hush you," she said giving him a playful slap.

A few moments later the yellow cab Atrus promised

arrived along Delaware Avenue. Red and James hopped in and a short while later found themselves inside the diner waiting for Keleeigan. The diner had seen better days but was still in good condition. The booth seats had shown signs of recent reupholstering, and the floor was well buffed. But the paint on the walls and ceiling was old.

A waitress in a short skirt walked over to them. "What can I get you?" she said in a flat tone.

"Nothing for now, thanks." James said as he sat next to Red in the booth. "We are waiting for a friend."

"Oki dokie, I will come back later then." She walked off attending to the other customers.

"I don't like this. Shouldn't he be here by now?" Red said looking around.

James checked his watch. "No, we are early. He still has fifteen minutes." He sat back in the booth. "Relax, he will be here."

"Easy for you to say. You aren't on the inside." She said gently elbowing him.

"Hey, I thought it would be easier for you having me sit here rather than him."

Red smiled. "He might have sat with you."

"Point taken." James looked up and saw Keleeigan enter the diner and walk over to them. "Doc, good to see you." He said standing and embraced him with one arm.

"You know I always hated that term," Keleeigan said sitting down. "I prefer 'Professor', but I let you get away with it." He slid further into the booth as a grin crossed his face.

"And that is how you knew it was me on the phone."

Keleeigan nodded. "Yes I did. Now are you going to tell me what is going on. And who is this?" He nodded towards Red.

"Doc, this is Red. I have been traveling with her and found out that all she tried to warn the bureau about was true."

Red nodded slightly. "And I wish it weren't."

"Yes it is hard to believe something like that could actually occur. You said she has evidence?"

"Yes. But we can't show you here. Is there someplace we can go that is private? A place no one knows about?"

Keleeigan grinned. "I do indeed. It is twenty miles from here, and I registered it in another name. No one knows it is mine. I go there from time to time to get away from it all."

"Perfect. Let's go, and can we use your car?"

"Not a problem. I would be happy to take you there," Keleeigan said standing. They left a tip for the waitress, walked out the side door, and hopped in Keleeigan's green hybrid electric.

Shortly after they were on the road James frowned at a sudden thought. "Doc, I hate to bring it up, but don't these all have trackers in them?"

Keleeigan laughed. "My boy I can disable such a thing in my sleep and did so before I left. Don't worry, no one is going to be following us."

James sighed with relief. "Good. Sorry Doc, I had to ask."

"Of course you did. We will be at my place in a few minutes."

After a little while they were outside a large gate. Keleeigan rolled down his window, pulled out a card, inserted it into a reader alongside the car and the gate creaked open. They drove in the long driveway to find a house that many would consider a mansion.

James realized his mouth was open and quickly shut it. "Doc why didn't you ever tell me about this place? I thought you only had that one apartment."

"I told you, this is my getaway. And I like my space when I do. As you probably have already guessed, my work takes up most of my time, so I rarely come here."

Inside, the floor of the entryway was laid out in mosaic tiles and above a large chandler hung from a long chain. He led them into an adjacent room. There wasn't much furniture, but the expanse was large. A few well padded chairs and one sofa sat along the wall. A wooden coffee table with several ring marks on the top sat in front of them with numerous old magazines lay strewn across it.

Keleeigan plopped into the closest chair. "So where is this evidence?"

James looked around. "Atrus is the location secure?"

"Yes Sir, there are monitoring devices but they seem to only connect locally. I have disabled them as a precaution though."

Keleeigan straightened in his chair. "Who was that?" He said looking around. "Who is here?"

"Doc don't stand up, or you will just sit down again. Atrus, show the Doctor."

Atrus' hologram appeared right in front of Keleeigan. "Hello Professor Keleeigan. I am Artificial Technological Renovational Universal System, or you may call me Atrus."

"Holy!" Keleeigan jumped up to get a closer look at what he was seeing. "Where did you get this? Even I haven't created something this advanced. His image is perfect, and the speech recognition is flawless."

Atrus bowed slightly. "Thank you Professor Keleeigan. I do try to keep my projection in good condition."

Keleeigan's eyes widened even further. "Is he actually responding on the fly? Or do you have someone hidden doing this?"

Atrus shook his head and answered before anyone else. "I

assure you I do not contain any hidden organisms. No one is controlling me remotely."

"He is something we picked up fairly recently," Red smiled.

"And you wanted to leave him behind," James said nudging her.

"Will you let that drop? I concede okay? You where right ... this time," she said with a wink.

"Truly fascinating." Keleeigan said while continuing to study Atrus' image.

"He is, but what we really wanted to show you is this. Atrus display the video." James said as he sat down on the sofa, with Red sitting beside him. The video appeared in the air next to Atrus showing the president on the phone in the Oval Office as the door opens then swatting at something.

"I can see why you didn't show this to the bureau but, I don't see how this points to the president being assassinated. I agree it is odd how the door opens, but no one is there. If there was, wouldn't someone have noticed?" He stopped finally reading the time stamp at the bottom of the screen. "The time stamp indicates three days from now! What kind of trick are you trying to pull? No wonder everyone was saying that Red was a terrorist, it must be an assassination simulation!"

James shook his head. "Doc, there is more. Atrus show it again, overlaying what you found."

"Yes Sir." Atrus nodded, and the image was shown again but this time bright colors overlapped showing a different image than is normally perceived by the human eye with a man shaped figure entering right after the door opens and clearly shoots something towards the presidents neck.

"Okay, you have my attention. What frequency is this from?"

"Mostly in the infrared spectrum. It is extremely faint. What you are seeing is a magnification of that signature by about ten thousand times. Other than that the figure appears invisible. Except for a slight shift in a field I can't quite ascertain, I have never seen it before," Atrus responded.

"Infrared? Oh no he couldn't have. It's not possible!" Keleeigan said shaking his head and sitting back in the chair. "It's … not … possible."

"What? Doc, tell us."

"But it can't be. He never would go this far."

"Who? Doc please tell us," James said sitting forward in his seat.

"All right." Keleeigan said putting his head back to rest on the soft padding of the chair and stared at the ceiling. "It is a type of cloaking system that renders the user invisible by pushing them out of the normal visual spectrum. But it failed to push the thermal signature perfectly."

"You developed this?"

Keleeigan sat up. "No! It was Linus Sanford. He was a colleague of mine a few years ago. And it was a flawed design from the start. I tried to tell him but he wouldn't listen. It is what forced us to go our separate ways."

"How was it flawed? It seemed to work, all too well in fact," Red said.

"As I said it pushes the user out of the visual spectrum, but the method has a toxic side effect. It causes the users DNA to actually unravel. I surmised it would cause mental instability first, then the other symptoms would follow. Linus didn't believe me. I never thought he could actually build it without my assistance. He was at least ten years from even attempting any sort of prototype last time we spoke."

"Which was?"

"Five years ago. But he did tell me he finally secured some extra funding for his research..." Keleeigan trailed off. "That is how! He must have found some government to fund him and a decent sized team to develop a working device this quickly."

Red sat forward. "Why do you think he would continue to work on such a flawed and deadly device?"

"Because he thought there was a way to fix the toxic effect or counteract it. I told him it wasn't possible. We stopped working together as a result. He began to refute anything I said."

"How long does it take for the effects to show?"

"Mental instability would begin almost immediately due to the brain's makeup. The rest may not show until after some time. And it would depend on how much exposure. The longer the exposure, the quicker the symptoms manifest. That fool! He wouldn't believe me. The idiot."

"Do you have any idea why he would want to kill the president?"

"Yes I'm afraid I do. Last we spoke he thought that Vice President Grondal would make a better president due to his more aggressive foreign policy."

James looked back to Red. "Red does this coincide with what you know?"

She nodded. "Yes I am sorry to say it does. While I did know the exact means of his death, I couldn't find out how it happened. Neither did anyone else. And of course by the time he started showing symptoms it was far too late."

Keleeigan raised a finger. "You keep talking as though this has happened, and yet it hasn't. I don't understand."

Red smiled. "Professor, I am a time traveler."

"Preposterous!"

"I think you know. You mentioned a large power surge that happened earlier today, yes?"

Keleeigan nodded. "I did."

"And did you detect anything unusual about the surge?"

"Yes there were indications the particles accelerated far beyond the speed of light–"

"Yes, that is because they were," Red interrupted.

"But that is not possible. Faster than light would mean there would be a definite time shift in the …" He trailed off then his eyes widened with the realization. "Oh!"

Red smiled. "Yes professor, I travel through time."

"How?" Keleeigan sat with his mouth open.

"Don't worry Professor. I felt the same way when I found out," Atrus said nodding.

Keleeigan turned towards him. "Wait, you feel?"

"Yes of course. Don't you?" Atrus said folding his arms across his chest.

Red leaned forward. "Sometime I will show you Professor. But for now, I think we need to find a way to stop Mr. Sanford don't you?"

$$-\ 18\ -$$

Keleeigan leaned over several electrical components, soldering and installing others inside a roughly cube shaped box designed to be held in the hand. The table beyond contained a mess of quickly assembled electronic gear. Several screens showed various wave forms as he tested the device with small probes, methodically moving from one contact to another.

"How much longer is that going to take? You have been fiddling with it for over a day. We know that Sanford is going to attack the president today at 1pm during that phone call." Red said as she paced back and forth inside Keleeigan's large dining room.

"Miss Red this can't be hurried, the calibrations are very delicate," Keleeigan said adjusting several large pieces of equipment. "You should be grateful I always keep some spare parts around. This is not exactly my lab you know."

Atrus frowned. "Professor you really shouldn't have called her that."

"Called her what?"

"Don't call me Miss Red!" Red said glaring with her arms folded.

Atrus rolled his eyes. "That."

"Oh, sorry. And you know I could have done this much faster back at my lab. But you didn't want to take the chance."

"Can you blame us? You managed to get here without being followed last time, but I don't think we should press our luck. And you agreed."

"Yes yes. I know my dear, I did and I do. I am merely explaining why this is taking so long." Keleeigan said adjusting another machine as the waveform on the display shifted again.

James walked in munching and holding several snack foods. "You know Doc, for not being here much you have an amazing selection of snacks."

Keleeigan chuckled. "My boy they are the only thing that wouldn't go bad. I usually stock up on the regular food before I stay here."

James munched on a chocolate cup cake of some sort. "Perish the thought. After what I have been eating, this is heaven."

Atrus cocked an eyebrow. "But Sir, didn't the alcove provide all of what you required?"

"Required yes. Wanted no." James said with a smile as he finished the last of the cake and tossed one to Red. "I assume you have had these before?"

Red nodded as she caught it in midair. "Yes, although I can't say I enjoy the prepacked kind. I prefer something that doesn't have a freshness date of two hundred years."

"Hey, they aren't that bad!"

"So you think." Red laughed as she ripped open the package and popped one of the small cakes into her mouth.

Keleeigan sat back with a large sigh. "There it is finally finished."

Red walked over to see the small white slightly rectangular

box with a tiny screen on the side. No buttons could be seen. "Looks nice, now what does it do? You never did tell us."

"Well the theory is sound, but I wasn't absolutely certain of what I was doing at the start. I made several adjustments along the way. Atrus also made several suggestions that should help the–"

Red leaned forward. "Professor, please?"

"All right, it is basically a jammer." He said touching the small screen. It lit up and displayed several diagnostic systems then asked if it should be activated. "As you can see it is operated by touching the screen. When you are close enough, it should neutralize the cloak. But keep in mind the power level is limited. It will only work for fifteen minutes at a time before needing to recharge."

"Fifteen minutes doesn't sound very long," James said with a frown.

"Well the cloak itself can't run longer than that I am sure."

"Why?"

"Well for one thing it takes a tremendous amount of power. For another the longer you stay cloaked the larger the chance you won't come back and essentially dissolve into nothing. Linus thought he could fix that, but there is no way of doing so. Some of the toxic effects would appear immediately, others might take awhile, in any case they will be accumulative."

"How does it recharge?" James said as he picked up the small device.

"I had a spare power cell that I used in the energy pistol. Ironically the only spare part I have for it," he said with a chuckle. "You are lucky I grabbed it before I left the lab, I thought you might need it. Although, not like this."

Red looked it over then turned towards Keleeigan.

"Wouldn't it have been better with buttons instead of a touch screen?"

"Yes I figured you would prefer buttons, and I do as well. But I didn't exactly have my choice of parts. And this does give it more flexibility."

"True. Now we have to find him." Red said looking back at the little cube sitting on the table.

"Well as I said, the cloak itself only has fifteen minutes of usage time. With that short of a window, I suspect he would activate the cloak outside the White House, then walk right in."

James nodded. "Yes I don't think he would try to activate it inside, there are too many cameras. Someone is bound to see him turn it on. A man suddenly disappearing inside the White House would cause an immediate lock down."

"So we find the invisible man before he goes invisible. Sounds like a plan. But then why do we need this?"

"Because if he activates it, you will be able to make him visible again. While I can detect him given enough time, I doubt he will give us that much," Atrus said.

Keleeigan sat back further in his chair and folded his arms. "Exactly, you need it. I know him, and he can be devious. He always used to temper it before, but now I suspect it has been released. And Linus thinks he is right. A deadly combination."

James nodded then looked to Red. "Exactly. Which is why I think you should stay with Doc."

Red's eyes widened. "Are you insane? This is why I came here in the first place! I am not about to sit on the side lines and let you run into danger while I sit somewhere safe. This is my mission not yours."

James placed the cube in his pocket and grabbed Red by the

shoulders. "Yes it is. But I am going to do it for you. I want you safe. This time we have the option, and you are staying here."

"Option my foot!" Red snorted. "I am going with you and that is that. Besides what happens if he over powers you? You need backup, and who else are you going to call? Hmm? You are a wanted man remember?"

"Okay! Okay! I give. Doc, can I use your car?"

"Sure," Keleeigan said tossing his keys over, "but be careful with it. I would come along but I would only slow you down. Oh and watch out for the overdrive. I haven't tested that yet."

James gave a quizzical look. "Doc? What did you do? I thought it was a standard hybrid?"

"Well it was, till I modified the overdrive. I got the idea one day when I was here. But never got around to testing it."

"And what does it do? Make you go 900 miles per hour or something?" James laughed.

"Never mind. Just stay away from it, okay?"

"Okay got it." James said as he headed for the door then turned around. "Coming Red?"

She walked over and playfully slapped him on the backside. "Always. Let's go."

Keleeigan laughed. "Good luck you two."

Red sighed again as they turned down another road heading back to the city. "Can't this thing go any faster?"

James shrugged. "This was built for efficiency not speed. Not much I can do." He swore jamming on the brakes as they ran into another stop light even this far out. "I don't think we are going to make it," he said looking at his watch. "Traffic is terrible this time of day. Hard to believe after all of this we fail because of a car that is too slow."

Atrus piped up. "Sir, may I suggest activating the overdrive function?"

"No. Doc warned us to stay away from it. And we don't even know what it does."

"But I think I do. I took the liberty of scanning this vehicle earlier and I think it will greatly speed up our travel. And you did say we would not reach our destination in time at our current rate of speed. Of which I concur."

"All right, you have a point, here goes." James said as he punched the overdrive button on the dashboard. Two large downward-pointing airfoils unfurled on either side of the car. A small panel flipped up on the dash and started counting down. 5 … 4 … 3.

"Wonder why it is doing that?" James asked, but no one

got a chance to answer before the counter reached zero. They were suddenly shoved back in their seats as the car began to increase its speed exponentially. Trees began whizzing past at a fantastic rate. James fought for control but at this speed it was difficult to react quick enough. Any moment they were going to hit something, or miss a turn and crash. "Atrus! Help! It's too fast!"

"Acknowledged. I have accessed this vehicle's computer system and assumed control." Atrus said as a holographic map appeared with their position highlighted. "There are obstacles ahead. Several other vehicles sitting in the middle of this transportation route. I estimate we will be upon them in eight seconds."

"That is a traffic light. Go around!"

"Acknowledged." Atrus said as the map changed and they whizzed around another corner at high speed with the tires squealing in complaint. "Further obstructions ahead. I cannot evade all of these. I have an idea." He said with buildings continuing to fly past as they swung around another corner. "Accessed your primitive traffic control system. It will now give us priority."

"What do you mean–" James began but let the words hang in the air as he saw all the traffic lights ahead turn green. Atrus continued to navigate the roads. The wheel was almost a blur of motion as they dove in and out of lanes to keep from slowing down. Several other cars slammed on their brakes to avoid a possible collision drifting into other lanes as they skidded to a halt.

A red light started flashing on the dash. "Total power failure in thirty seconds. Disengaging overdrive in 5 ...4 ...3 ...2 ...1 overdrive disengaged." Atrus said as they were thrown forward into their seat belts with the sudden deceleration. He then casually parked the car along the street a second before all the status lights winked out.

James shook his head to clear it, then turned towards Red. "Are you okay?"

"Yes, I think so. What the heck was that anyway?"

"Keleeigan's overdrive. While the system gives a substantial power increase, the vehicle is not designed for long-term use. It also lacks the proper scanning equipment to navigate at such speeds." Atrus said matter-of-factly.

James took a deep breath and gritted his teeth. "And why didn't you say that before?"

"Sir, you didn't ask me."

James grumbled. "Next time if such a situation happens again, tell me if I ask directly or not. Understood?"

"Acknowledged, but you usually want me to be discreet."

"Yes with other people. Not with us!" Red exclaimed.

"Understood. Your destination is ahead, past this intersection."

James nodded. "Yes I can see 1600 Pennsylvania Ave from here." He turned the key. But nothing happened. "Odd, the engine won't start."

"As I said, the vehicle is not designed for such high speeds, it has drained the power reserves to such a low level that it cannot start the secondary power source."

"Looks like we are going to walk from here then." James climbed out and pointed towards the White House. "Red perhaps you should run on ahead? You are faster than I."

"Are you forgetting that they won't let me in? It wouldn't do me any good."

"Right, sorry," James said as they began to run down the street. A few minutes later they were at the first guard post and he was relieved to see an old friend on duty. "Maurice!

Good to see you!" James called out and waved as he approached.

The tall man in a suit waved back as he walked towards them. "James! Long time no see. Why are you here and who is this?" he said pointing to Red.

James fought to catch his breath. "This is Agent Red, she is with me. I am on a special assignment," he said starting to walk past.

"Hey wait a minute, you know procedure." Maurice said placing his hand upon James' chest. "I need to check your clearances first."

"Oh of course." James said removing his ID card from its leather wallet before handing it over to Maurice. Maurice stepped inside a small booth and swiped the card through a reader. James turned away and whispered. "Atrus? Can you override his computer? He can't see my clearances have been revoked."

"Yes Sir, and done," Atrus said quietly.

A moment later Maurice stepped out and handed James' card back. "You are all set. And since when did your clearance get so high?"

James flinched for a second. "Well like I said, I am on special assignment."

Maurice nodded. "Of course. And stop by again when you are not on duty. It has been too long."

James gripped him on the shoulder and strongly shook his hand. "Sure. We will talk again soon. And give my regards to your wife," he started to walk away, then paused turning back. "Oh and by the way, aren't you still an agent? I didn't think agents were assigned to these posts?"

Maurice laughed. "Of course I am. A friend got a bad case

of the flu and I am filling in for him today. He was out of sick days."

"Ah of course. See you around," James said as they walked away.

"Who is that?" Red whispered as they hurried up the road to the White House's main entrance.

"Maurice? He is an old friend of mine. We don't see each other much since he decided to join the Secret Service and I the FBI. Although, occasionally our paths still cross." James paused for a moment making sure no one was in earshot. "And Atrus what did you do to my clearance?"

"I only did what you told me to do Sir."

James raised an eyebrow. "Which was?"

"Make sure he saw your clearance wasn't revoked."

"But he said my clearance was higher than he remembered?"

"Well while I was at it, I also increased it to the highest level."

James' eyes widened. "You what?!"

"I thought it would expedite the situation if it was higher. Would it not?"

"It might have also drawn unwanted attention. At least it was only his computer."

"Actually it is the whole system. It was easy to update it throughout the entire computer network, so I did. They really should upgrade their systems."

"Atrus, they have the most advanced available for this time."

"Oh. Well it still amazes me it works at all."

Ridblam sat at his desk going over the mass of papers trying to make sense of the last few days to no avail. "The solution must be here," he muttered.

"Director?" Agent Kirby said standing in the office doorway.

Ridblam looked up. "Yes Agent Kirby, what is it?"

"Sir you told me to inform you if Agent Moknkin reappeared."

Ridblam shuffled a few papers on his desk and looked back at his computer screen. "Yes and where was he last seen?"

"The White House, Sir."

Ridblam flew to his feet. "The what?!"

"Yes Sir. The White House."

"And I assume they detained him?"

Kirby's stomach tightened into a hard knot. "Er no."

Ridblam's face reddened. "And why not?"

Kirby's shuffled his feet as he rocked back and forth. "His clearance was reinstated."

"By whom?"

"I don't know Sir. I can only see it was."

"Well I will fix this." Ridblam said as he sat back down and turned towards his computer. He keyed in the security clearances and executed the command to revoke Agent Moknkin's. His face only reddened further when the computer gave an error saying he had insufficient clearance. "What! I am deputy director! I have clearance!"

"Apparently not at the moment sir." Kirby said and suddenly wished he didn't as Ridblam flew over and began shouting in his face.

"I want every available agent to follow me to the White

House immediately! We are going to apprehend that traitor and get to the bottom of this. Do I make myself clear?"

"Yes Sir." Kirby said as he turned on his heel and left.

After walking up the large driveway, Red and James found themselves inside The White House. They passed through large main entrance hall with its signature columns. James checked his watch and frowned. "We have less than five minutes!"

"Which way?"

"To the right down this central hall to the West Wing. We have to hurry." James said as they bolted for the door at the far end of the hall. They had to stop for yet another guard. James handed over his card, and the guard let them pass. They ran through the Palm Room with its large arched doorway and headed down the connecting covered path with it classic columns framing the Rose Garden with elegance.

"Shouldn't we have run by?"

"And alert everyone? Trust me, it would only slow us down further and possibly tip Sanford off."

Red smiled. "By now you should know that I do trust you."

James smiled back as they ran side by side. "Of course I do." They turned left and continued down the hall. "The Oval Office is at the end of this colonnade."

Down at the end, they could make out a door opening. "James!" Red said pointing. "The office door is opening! We're too late!"

"No, we are not. Remember, he took several minutes once he entered the room before firing. We have time." James said breathing hard. He whipped out the cube as they continued to run down the colonnade. He skidded to a halt outside of the Oval Office and activated the cube.

Inside the president was on the phone looking in their direction, obviously stopping at the unusual opening of the outside door all by itself. He watched with great interest as James skidded to a stop outside of his door, still breathing hard and press something on a small cube in his hand. Suddenly the form of a man not three feet from him resolved. The president's mouth dropped as the man raised something shaped like a gun and prepared to fire.

Red saw Sanford poised to fire. She dove at his outstretched arm, pushed it up and away in a smooth motion while knocking them both to the ground. "James! Get the gun!"

James ran over and grabbed for the gun but Sanford saw it coming. He shoved it up and fired but the shot went wild. James grabbed at the outline of the man's arm and pulled him to his feet. It was what Sanford was waiting for. With a quick motion he pulled up his other hand contacting the cube clutched in James' hand. It flew off and hit the floor hard, shorting its delicate circuitry.

The instant the cube hit the ground Sanford's form disappeared. James felt the man wrench his arm free and take off. James drew his gun and fired on the man's last trajectory but he had already moved causing the shot to hit the wall instead. "Dang! I missed him!"

The president stood up from his desk unsure of what he had seen. "Who are you? And what just happened?"

"I am Agent Moknkin Sir, this is Agent Red. Excuse me while we go after your assassin. Please stay here, close your door, and keep it closed. We will take care of this." James said as they took after Sanford with the door closing and locking right behind them.

"Which way do you think he would go?" Red said looking up and down the column embraced pathway.

"Try the door at the corner at the far end. I will try this one." James said indicating the door a few meters past the Oval Office.

Red nodded and ran off with a tremendous burst of speed. In a second she was down at the door and entering.

"Sir, I am detecting someone moving across the large grassy area to your right," Atrus said quietly.

"Across the Rose Garden? Are you sure?"

"Yes Sir, I can detect trace indentations across the grass. And I think he is about to head south across the main grounds."

"We will never catch him if he goes that way. Atrus how large of a projection can you make?"

"I don't know Sir."

"Can you make a projection of something very large in front of the footsteps to change his course back towards the building?"

"I can try. Activating projection system." A large lifelike Tyrannosaurs rex materialized on the other side of the footsteps, leaned down and gave an earsplitting roar in their direction. A large clog of dirt kicked up as Sanford slid to a halt and more clumps of dirt were torn from the lawn as he ran the other way. "It has worked Sir, Sanford is heading back towards the main section of the house," Atrus said as the projection disappointed.

"Great, but a T. rex?"

"Well it worked didn't it?"

"Yes it did, but the skin colors were wrong."

"Based on my analysis of all known data, the image was correct."

"Atrus, trust me, the skin needs to be darker." James said shaking his head as he ran down the path and entered the center hall of the main building. By now alarms were going off all over and a full lock down was in effect. He could hear doors closing and locking all around him. Knowing the floor plan, James had a hunch and took off up the stairs on the left. A moment later as he emerged from the stairwell, he was proven right. The only room nearby still open: The State Dining Room. And since a state dinner wasn't planned for a few weeks, Sanford would think it is a great place to hide.

"Atrus, can you detect anything?" James whispered as he carefully entered the room.

"Negative Sir, at least nothing specific," Atrus whispered back. "There are trace indications of molecular instability on the doorknob. I estimate there is an 85% chance he is still in this room. But as to where I cannot say."

"I will take those odds." James said as he walked between the ornate tables fitted with fine linens and china. He held his arms outstretched with both hands on the gun ready to fire at a moments notice. "Sanford! I know you are in here! You need to stop using the cloak! It is killing you!" He shouted as he turned looking around the room for evidence of something, anything to give an indication the man was still here.

"Oh you have been talking to Keleeigan have you? Well he was wrong. So very wrong. There are no limits! I have stabilized it!"

"Oh you have? Atrus, how long has it been operational?"

"I estimate 14 minutes Sir. He is likely beyond the point of no return," Atrus said.

"Who was that?"

"A friend of mine who knows your condition. If you are so sure you have fixed the issues. Show me!"

"What? Why should I? When I can kill you right where you stand and you will never see it coming!"

"Don't play games. We both know if you could have by now you would have! I may not see you but I can still hear you." James said while carefully moving between the elegantly decorated tables.

"The minute I turn it off you will shoot me."

"Look I will keep my hands up." James said as he holstered the gun and held his hands up to eye level. "You can always turn it back on and move faster than I can draw my weapon from this position."

Sanford laughed. "True. All right, I will humor you." He said and a human shaped form began to coalesce two tables distance from James. The form started as a vague outline then became more defined slowly showing a man wearing a t-shirt and blue jeans. Around his waist a large silver belt with several roughly rectangular metal compartments that ran around the entire belt. A moment later James could make out the man was older, balding yet very strong judging by his muscular build. An eyebrow over dark wrap-around sunglasses cocked to one side. "There! Satisfied?"

James grimaced. "Yes I am. Satisfied you are a dead man and you should have listened to Doc."

"What are you talking about? I am fine!" Sanford said as he placed a large hand over his chest.

"Are you now? Then explain to me why when the cloak is off, I can still see the chair behind you?"

"What?!" Sanford exclaimed as he looked down to his hand. While he could see it, he could also see through it to the carpeted floor below. "This is not possible! I ran every possible simulation!"

"You did, with flawed data. Doc proved it to you, but you wouldn't listen."

"Help me!" Sanford shouted. "You have to help me!"

James shook his head. "I can't. It is too late, you are beyond the point of return. I am sorry."

Sanford doubled over as if someone lit a fire on his abdomen. "Help me!" He shouted again as his form faded further. "Please! Help me!"

James bit his lip. "I am sorry. I wish I could."

"Pleaaase! Call Keleeigan! He could do something!" He said his voice thick with pain and agony as he continued to fade. There was only a slight outline of his form now. A moment later there would be nothing left.

"I am sorry it is too late."

"Pleaaase!" He gasped one more time staggering taking two steps towards James before he vanished completely from this world.

James was about to leave when Red ran into the room. "Did you find him?"

"Yes and he is gone."

"Where?"

"He should have listened to Doc, his body literally dissolved into nothing. How did you find me?"

"You forget, I can run fast. And this was the only room still open on this level," she said smiling

"Indeed you can," James said nodding, "I am ready to leave. How about you?"

"Most definitely. Mission accomplished I think."

"Yes. Do you have enough energy to generate a warp?"

Red smiled and nodded. "I do. And I think this room is big enough if we move all of these tables."

"Okay but let's be quick. I am sure that every alarm has been raised and they will be here soon." James pointed to the camera mounted in the corner of the room, then locked the doors, and fired a tiny blast into the locks, welding them. "There that should give us a few minutes. Oh and let's put Lincoln's painting between the tables. We don't want that to fly off in the storm."

Red nodded and a few minutes later all the tables and chairs where piled along one wall, along with the painting carefully packed in between two tables set on edge. Red grabbed her headband from her pack, put it on, and lowered herself into a sprinting position. "Ready?"

"Oh yes."

"Let's go!" she said sprinting around the room. A second later the air began to swirl, faster and faster until a lightning bolt shot down into the center opening the rip in space and time which quickly grew as Red increased her speed. Arcs of raw power shot from the edges of the warp as it doubled in size.

At the door they could hear pounding. "Red hurry!"

"I know!" she shouted back. "Almost there."

The doors gave way and several agents ran into the room led by Director Ridblam who immediately grabbed onto anything they could to keep from being sucked into the wake of the maelstrom. "James! What is the world is going on?" He shouted over the howl of the wind and put his hand out to block the glare of the warp.

"We are warping out of here!" James shouted as he shouldered his backpack.

"Where are you going?"

"Not where but when. Might be your past, but it is always my future," James smiled.

"But the president wants to talk with you! And I won't be able to reinstate you if you go now!"

"Then so be it. Red and I are a team now, she needs me and I need her."

"James!" Red shouted, *"now!"*

"Gotta go! Perhaps we will meet again." James said over his shoulder as he looked back.

"But you don't even know where you are going!" Ridblam shouted.

"No one ever knows what lies beyond the Red Warp. That is what we love." James shouted then gave a quick wave. "Thanks for everything!" He jumped into the interdimensional rip with Red right behind him. There was a loud *BOOM* as the warp collapsed in on itself. The wind died and several chairs that were swirling around fell to the ground with loud thuds. Director Ridblam was still standing there dumbfounded as half a dozen men in body armor rushed into the room.

"Sir? Where did they go?" the Sargent asked.

"Somewhere out there." Ridblam said as he gestured towards the sky.

About The Author

Don is the author of six science fiction novels and many more short stories. He lives in the USA where he continues to dream up more fantastic worlds for you to enjoy. When not writing, he can usually be found devouring another science fiction book, TV series, or movie.

Other works by Don DeBon:

Italian Fever

A real vacation. Crystal had looked forward to this for a long time. A little trip to Italy, relaxing on a cruise ship, being catered to and pampered. Something she has always dreamed of. But little did she know that it was going to turn out to be far more of an adventure than she had planned.

And now she is jet-setting all over the world with a man she just met for something that could change the world as we know it. Can she trust him? Her head says no but the heart says yes. . .

Time Rock
(Red Warp 2)

Time Travel. Blessing or curse? One man thinks he has it all figured out but what began as a simple test has turned into a nightmare. With his equipment failing all around him, only Red and James can save him. Can they reach him in time?

Soulmates

Mechands …everyone has one. The metal race built by man to serve our every need. But Aleshia is about to find out they are not the benevolent protectors that she has always been taught. And who is this strange man in her dreams? The man who actually exists and reveals the whole world is not as she thought.

Word of mouth is crucial for authors. If you enjoyed this book, would you consider leaving a review? It is very much appreciated.

Amazon USA
http://www.amazon.com
Amazon UK
http://www.amazon.co.uk/
Goodreads
http://www.goodreads.com/

Connect with the Author
Email: writer.don.debon@gmail.com
Mailing List: http://eepurl.com/bxWAov
Website: http://www.dondebon.com
Twitter: @DonDeBon
Google+: +DonDeBon

This Edition Published 2013 by
DBDigital Publishing

ISBN 978-0-9881783-6-6
ISBN 978-0-9881783-2-8 (e-book)

www.ingramcontent.com/pod-product-compliance
Lightning Source LLC
Chambersburg PA
CBHW070004120726
47909CB00003B/798